"Where's Gretchen's father?"

Frannie had thought her heart would stop when she'd dodged Travis's question. Guilt had swept through her. She realized she should have told him years ago that their single night of passion hadn't been without results. However, at the time, she'd thought her reasons for not telling him were sound.

She wasn't about to remain in Cooperville so he could play father. Certainly, if he'd wanted her to stay all those years ago, wanted a future with her, he would have asked her to stay and build a life with him on that last night together....

Besides, Travis had been inundated with responsibility, taking care of his sick mother and his younger sisters. He hadn't needed one more burden. Now it no longer mattered. Too much time had passed for her to release the secret. Besides, the truth would only complicate everyone's lives...wouldn't it?

Dear Reader,

This month, Silhouette Romance is celebrating the classic love story. That intensely romantic, emotional and compelling novel you just can't resist. And leading our month of classic love stories is *Wife without a Past* by Elizabeth Harbison, a deeply felt tale of an amnesiac wife who doesn't recognize the FABULOUS FATHER she'd married....

Pregnant with His Child... by bestselling author Carla Cassidy will warm your heart as a man is reunited with the child he never knew existed—and the woman he never stopped loving. Next, our MEN! promotion continues, as Silhouette Romance proves a good man isn't hard to find in *The Stranger's Surprise* by Laura Anthony. In Patricia Thayer's moving love story, *The Cowboy's Convenient Bride,* a woman turns up at a Texas ranch with a very poignant secret. And in *Plain Jane Gets Her Man* by Robin Wells, you'll be delighted by the modern-day Cinderella who wins the man of her dreams. Finally, Lisa Kaye Laurel's wonderful miniseries, ROYAL WEDDINGS, continues with *The Prince's Baby.*

As the Thanksgiving holiday approaches, I'd like to give a special thanks to all of you, the readers, for making Silhouette Romance such a popular and beloved series of books. Enjoy November's titles!

Regards,

Melissa Senate
Senior Editor
Silhouette Books

Please address questions and book requests to:
Silhouette Reader Service
U.S.: 3010 Walden Ave., P.O. Box 1325, Buffalo, NY 14269
Canadian: P.O. Box 609, Fort Erie, Ont. L2A 5X3

Books by Carla Cassidy

Silhouette Romance

Patchwork Family #818
Whatever Alex Wants... #856
Fire and Spice #884
Homespun Hearts #905
Golden Girl #924
Something New #942
Pixie Dust #958
The Littlest Matchmaker #978
The Marriage Scheme #996
Anything for Danny #1048
*Deputy Daddy #1141
*Mom in the Making #1147
*An Impromptu Proposal #1152
*Daddy on the Run #1158
Pregnant with His Child... #1259

Silhouette Intimate Moments

One of the Good Guys #531
Try To Remember #560
Fugitive Father #604
Behind Closed Doors #778

*The Baker Brood

Silhouette Desire

A Fleeting Moment #784
Under the Boardwalk #882

Silhouette Shadows

Swamp Secrets #4
Heart of the Beast #11
Silent Screams #25
Mystery Child #61

Silhouette Books

*Silhouette Shadows
  Short Stories* 1993
"Devil and the Deep Blue Sea"

The Loop

Getting it Right: Jessica

Yours Truly

Pop Goes the Question

CARLA CASSIDY

had her first Silhouette novel, *Patchwork Family*, published in September of 1991, and since that time Carla has written over twenty-five books for five Silhouette lines. She's looking forward to writing many more books and bringing hours of pleasure to her readers.

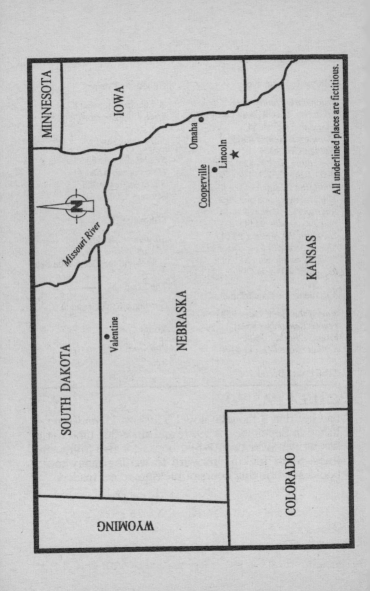

MINNESOTA

IOWA

Omaha

Lincoln

Cooperville

N

Missouri River

Valentine

SOUTH DAKOTA

NEBRASKA

KANSAS

WYOMING

COLORADO

All underlined places are fictitious.

Prologue

Travis Richards stood at the edge of the cornfield, watching the small two-story farmhouse nearby. Surely Frannie wouldn't really leave. Surely last night she'd just been talking, dreaming, like she had so many nights before.

Overhead, the moon was full, spilling down light that painted the surrounding farmland in soft silvery hues. The scent of the summer corn surrounded him, but couldn't dispel the memory of the sweet fragrance of Frannie that still clung to his skin.

Last night, they'd finally made love, and it had been everything he dreamed of, as wondrous as he anticipated.

She can't leave, he thought desperately.

He held his wristwatch up to the moonlight. Nearly midnight.

"I'm leaving at midnight tomorrow night, Travis," she'd said as she lay in his arms the night before. "If you're coming with me, be here then. I'll only wait a minute or two for you.''

How could she even think of leaving now...after what they had shared? Travis closed his eyes, remembering the warmth of her body against his, the sweet moans she'd breathed into the hollow of his neck as he possessed her completely. All day long he'd tried to figure out how to stop her, wondered what he could do to make her stay.

The sound of a window being raised made him snap his eyes open. Frannie's bedroom window. Suddenly he remembered the very first time he'd seen Frannie. He was eleven at the time. He'd heard a ten-year-old girl had come to live on the neighboring farm, and he'd snuck out of the house late one night to see if he could catch a glimpse of this new girl.

He'd stood in this very same place, hidden in the high stalks of corn, and watched in fascination as a pair of skinny legs extended out the second-story window. The legs cast about, the toes obviously seeking some sort of foothold on the wooden rose trellis.

Eventually the legs were followed by the rest of the body, a tiny sprite of a girl with long dark hair. She'd hit the ground, looked around with a sense of satisfaction, then returned up the trellis and disappeared back into the house.

In the eight years Frannie lived here, she'd often escaped out the window, first to sneak away from her stern grandfather, then, later, to run to Travis's arms.

With the loud thud of a suitcase hitting the ground, Travis was yanked from the past and into the present. Frannie's legs were tanned and shapely, although she was still small and petite. With years of practice, she nimbly descended the trellis and picked up her suitcase.

Travis took a step backward, farther into the corn, knowing that if she saw him she'd assume he was coming with her. And for him, leaving was impossible.

Frannie looked around expectantly, her body appearing to vibrate with energy and excitement. *Don't go.* Travis's heart spoke the words he couldn't verbalize. For the first time ever, he hoped her grandfather would wake up. Poppy would rant and rave and insist Frannie get back inside. At least it would buy Travis some time to change her mind.

However, Poppy's head didn't appear at any window, nor did any lights go on to indicate the old man had awakened. As usual, Frannie had successfully snuck out.

With a lump in his throat, Travis watched as she looked at her watch, then once again gazed out in his direction. He knew she couldn't see him, but his heart continued to bang frantically against his ribs.

She'd believed he would go with her. And always before, when she needed him, he'd been right by her side. But not this time. This time he had to let her go alone, no matter how he ached to be with her. Duty battled desire within him. His mind filled with a vision of his frail mother, his two young sisters. He was all they had. No matter how he wanted to run away with Frannie, no matter how he ached to throw all his duties and responsibilities aside, he couldn't.

As if to confirm that very fact, his mother had suffered an especially bad time that day, as if she somehow knew he was wavering between going and staying. Seeing his mother so weak and helpless had made his decision final. He had to stay.

Frannie looked at her watch again, her shoulders slightly slumped. She'd always been impatient. She hated waiting for anything or anyone.

Oh, he wanted to escape his hiding place, run to her and insist she stay here with him in Cooperville. He wanted to make love to her over and over again, until she forgot her driving desire to leave this small Nebraska town.

His heart sank as he saw her tighten her grip on her suitcase handle and straighten her shoulders with determination.

"Travis?" Her soft voice rode the night wind to where he stood hidden. "Travis? Are you here?"

He held his breath, not wanting to give her false hope, afraid that she might change his mind, that she would talk him into leaving with her. Leaving was impossible, but he hadn't realized until this moment that staying here without her would be utterly unbearable.

"I'm going now." She hesitated one more moment, then took off across the yard.

Don't go. Pain shot through his heart as he watched her leave the yard and reach the road that ran in front of the farm. Tears burned at his eyes, and he swallowed convulsively to hold them back.

The moonlight shone fully on her as she walked away, her footsteps firm and determined against the gravel surface. With each step her silhouette got smaller, less visible. A cloud skittered in front of the moon, momentarily obscuring the lunar light. When it passed, she was gone.

For a long moment, Travis remained still, unable to believe she had really left. She was gone from Cooperville. Gone from him. "Frannie." He whispered her name softly, as if by doing so he could pull her back to him. But his heart pounded with a profound emptiness and in that echoing emptiness, was the knowledge that his best friend really was gone. And he knew Frannie well enough to know that unless something beyond her control occurred, she would not be back. Not ever.

Chapter One

Five years later

"Poppy, I'm home."

Francine Webster stood in the doorway of the darkened house, waiting for a sign of welcome from the old man who sat in the rocking chair by the fireplace.

"So you are." His voice resembled the creak of the rocker, low and rumbling, as if functioning beneath an enormous weight.

Francine sighed and realized she'd been foolish to think that her grandfather would be pleased to see her. He hadn't liked her much five years ago, when she decided to leave him and this town behind. And she had a feeling that her forced return, because she was flat broke, with an illegitimate child and a mongrel puppy, wouldn't improve their tenuous relationship either.

She shoved a strand of dark hair off her forehead,

exhausted from the long trip. Never again would she attempt a seventeen-hour trip in a twenty-five-year-old car with an energetic four-year-old child beside her and a puppy in a box in the back seat. She now looked behind her for her daughter. "Gretchen, come and say hello to your great-grandfather," she instructed.

The dark-haired little girl approached where the old man sat. The room was suddenly silent as he stopped rocking and returned her steady gaze. "Hello, Poppy. It's a pleasure to meet you," she said, mouthing the words Francine had spent at least an hour teaching her.

The old man wrinkled his brow. "How do you know it's a pleasure to meet me? Maybe I'm mean and hateful and you won't like me at all."

Gretchen stared at him for a long moment, then displayed her smile of sunshine. "'Course I will. And you can't be mean and hateful, 'cause you're my very own special grandpa."

He cleared his throat in surprise, his bushy eyebrows pulling together to meet across his brow in one long, unbroken line. "It's past bedtime." He didn't quite meet Francine's gaze. "I put a cot for the girl in your old bedroom." The rocker resumed its creaking, this time a bit more rapidly, and Francine knew from experience that was his way of dismissing her.

"Come on, pumpkin, it's been a long day, and we need to get our things from the car." With a weary sigh, she led Gretchen back outside.

The slam of the screen door evoked a thousand instant memories in Francine's mind. How many times in the splendid optimism of youth had she vowed that one day she'd hear that resounding bang for the very last time? And now it was with weary defeat that she heard it once again.

"Beauty!" Gretchen shoved the passenger seat forward and scrambled into the back, where the cardboard box quivered and shook, emitting short, ear-piercing yips. Gretchen reached inside and withdrew the little pup, who appeared delighted at his freedom.

"I don't know how your grandfather is going to react to Beauty," Francine warned her daughter, eyeing the puppy skeptically.

Beauty was hardly a suitable name for the ugly little puppy they'd found in a garbage can in Central Park. Covered with scruffy black-and-white fur, with a nose that looked like it had hit one too many walls, the puppy had instantly crawled into Gretchen's heart.

"Oh, Poppy will get used to Beauty...just like he'll get used to me." Gretchen giggled as the dog stuck out a little pink tongue and licked her cheek.

As Francine pulled their meager belongings out of the trunk of the car, she marveled, as always, at the miracle of Gretchen. There were days when Francine knew her daughter had been given to her to save her sanity. Gretchen was a gift from heaven. The rest of Francine's life had been sent straight from hell.

As they walked back toward the house, the scent of honeysuckle was redolent on the summer night breeze. The shoulder-high corn whispered a familiar song, and for a moment she could hear the echo of laughter from the distant past. The memory of her own laughter and the deeper, rich sounds of masculine happiness flooded through her, bringing with it a bittersweet joy and an abiding sadness.

She looked out at the neighboring house. Although there was some distance between the nearest home and Poppy's, the two structures were close enough that a flashlight shone from one window as a signal could be seen from a person in the other house.

"Can she sleep with me?" Gretchen asked as they walked back toward the house.

The windows were dark. Nobody was home. She wondered if his family still lived there. Francine tried to ignore the pangs that thoughts of him always produced.

"Mommy?"

"What?" The honeysuckle scent wrapped around Francine, embracing her in distant memories... memories of undying passion and distant dreams... and Travis.

Gretchen's insistent tugging on Francine's shirttail brought Francine from her reverie. "So can she?" she asked.

"Can who what?" Francine asked, consciously pushing away the past and looking down at her daughter.

"Can Beauty sleep with me?"

Francine shook her head. "That's not a good idea. She'll have to sleep in the kitchen. We'll need to put down some newspapers, since she's not quite house-trained yet."

"She'll be so lonely." Beauty whimpered, as if to punctuate Gretchen's plaintive sentence.

Francine smiled at her daughter. "But she'll adjust very quickly. And you won't be lonely, because we're sharing my old bedroom. So I'll be your roomie."

Gretchen smiled happily. "I think I'm going to like

it here,'' she pronounced as they walked back into the front door.

The rocking chair was empty, the house quiet, as Francine and Gretchen went back through the living room. ''Where did Poppy go?'' Gretchen asked softly.

''He must have gone on to bed.''

''But he didn't kiss us good-night,'' Gretchen exclaimed with disappointment.

''Poppy really isn't the kissing type,'' Francine said, fighting off an old familiar resentment that created a tight ball in her chest.

Gretchen looked at her in amazement. ''Of course he's the kissing type,'' she protested. ''He's a grandpa.''

Francine bit back her retort and led the little girl up the stairs into the small bedroom where she had spent all of her childhood years. Except for the cot made up on one side of the room, everything looked exactly as she'd left it five years ago, when she left the small town behind to find something different...something better.

Francine set their suitcases just inside the door. ''Let's go take care of Beauty. Then I'll get you all tucked in,'' she said.

It took only moments for them to get Beauty settled in a corner of the kitchen. They placed papers on the floor, then used an old window screen Francine found on the porch to pen her in the small area near the stove.

''Okay, pumpkin, bedtime for you,'' Francine said. As they shut off the light and left the kitchen, Beauty whined a good-night.

"Are we gonna stay here, Mommy?" Gretchen asked after she crawled beneath the blankets on the cot and stifled a big yawn.

Francine sat down on the edge of the cot and brushed several strands of dark hair from Gretchen's forehead. "For a little while, at least." Francine needed to see about a job as soon as possible, get together some money so that they could leave once again.

"Was this really your room when you were a little girl like me?" Gretchen asked sleepily.

"It really was. I'd stand in front of that very dresser mirror and pretend that I was a famous actress. And I had a perfume bottle shaped like a microphone, and I'd sing and talk into it." Francine smiled when she realized Gretchen had fallen sound asleep, her deep breaths plumping her baby cheeks as she exhaled.

Francine undressed, then pulled on her own over-size sleep shirt and stood in front of the old dresser mirror, staring at her image reflectively.

The dream-filled child she had once been was gone, along with the rebellious teenager whose only desire had been to escape from the small town and the rigid old man who'd raised her.

The woman who stared back at her was a stranger...a failure with defeat stamped on her features. Although she was only twenty-three years old, at the moment she felt fifty. Coming back here was the most difficult thing she'd ever done.

She straightened her shoulders and whirled away from the mirror. She wasn't defeated, she reminded herself firmly. She was just a little down on her luck. It was a temporary sort of thing, one she wouldn't admit to anyone except herself. She just needed some time and good fortune, then they'd head back to New York.

Without Gretchen, she would have never returned here, to this house and the town that held so many painful memories. She would have remained in New York, lived in her car...done whatever it took to seek her dreams.

However, Gretchen was her number one priority, and she couldn't ask her daughter to make the sacrifices that would be necessary had they remained in New York. Gretchen deserved a warm bed, good food, and the sun-filled summer days this place could provide.

When the money ran out and things fell apart, Francine had had no other alternative than to come back to the small midwestern town that had never embraced her and the old man who'd never been able to give her what she needed most.

Not for long, she promised herself. Staying here was only temporary. She hoped by the time fall came she would have enough money to return to New York and get Gretchen enrolled in a good school.

Besides, as far as the good people of Cooperville were concerned, she was a "star" coming home for a vacation. Francine wasn't about to admit failure to anyone. She'd let them think she was here to visit, to let Gretchen get to know her great-grandfather.

The bedroom was stuffy, the heat of the day trapped inside. Francine crossed the room and opened the window. Although the air coming in was warm, at least it was moving.

Exhausted, but too wound up to go directly to

sleep, she paced the room, finally stopping before a corkboard hanging on the wall. The board held high school memorabilia. She frowned. The sparse collection of keepsakes was a reminder of the fact that she had never really belonged. The town hadn't bothered with her, her grandfather hadn't wanted her here, and in the end, Travis hadn't wanted her, either.

"What you need is a nice glass of cold milk," she muttered. And I'll drink it straight from the carton, she thought with a touch of her old rebelliousness. Poppy had always hated her drinking from the carton...which was, of course, the reason she'd done it so often.

With a backward glance at her sleeping daughter, she shut off the bedroom light and padded down the stairs and into the dark kitchen. The tiny light in the refrigerator blinked on, as if to witness her subversive activity. She grabbed the plastic jug of milk, flipped the lid off with her thumb, then raised it to her lips.

"So, the prodigal granddaughter has returned."

Francine gasped in surprise at the deep voice. The milk jug tumbled from her hand to the floor. A splash of the cold liquid spewed her legs, then surrounded her feet. A soft bark of pleasure was followed by a lapping sound.

The light overhead blinked on, and she saw first the puppy at her feet, amid a sea of milk, then the man sitting at the table.

In an instant, her gaze encompassed him. He sat with one ankle resting on the other knee, the chair tipped precariously on the back legs. The blue jeans he wore were faded and contoured to an intimate fit. His white T-shirt stretched taut across the broad chest, the short sleeves baring strong, tanned arms. One hand was wrapped firmly around the bottle of beer resting on the table, the other was latched through his belt loop by a thumb.

"Travis...what are you doing here?" Francine asked in shocked surprise.

Suddenly the front legs of the chair hit the floor. "I usually come over every night and check on Poppy before going to bed."

Francine averted her gaze from him. She hadn't been prepared to face him yet, hadn't been ready for the instantaneous flare of heat the sight of him evoked or the onslaught of emotions he caused. She grabbed a roll of paper towels and began sopping up the mess on the floor, overly conscious of the shortness of her nightshirt. "I guess it won't be necessary for you to check on Poppy now that I'm home."

"I reckon I won't be changing my schedule just because you decided to breeze back into town." His tone held a slight edge of resentment, and Francine bit back an angry retort. She was too tired to fight with him, too disheartened at the moment to root around in the bitter fragments of their past.

As she picked up the puppy, she was very aware of his gaze on her. She flushed and busied herself arranging the screen so that Beauty couldn't make another escape, then finished cleaning the last of the milky mess on the floor.

The silence between them grew, filled with unspoken recriminations and the sour seeds of the distant past. He didn't attempt to break the tension. He sipped his beer, his stare never wavering from her, his expression dark and enigmatic.

He hasn't changed, Francine thought. It was as if the last five years had never happened, had not touched him at all.

With his black hair in need of a trim and his lower jaw shaded with a five-o'clock shadow, he still looked like the tough kid from the wrong side of the tracks she'd grown up with. He still looked like the boy who'd been her best friend, the teenager who'd been her champion and the man who'd been her lover for a single night. And the erratic beating of her heart at the sight of him angered her.

Finally, he finished the beer, tossed the bottle in the garbage pail and stood up. "I heard you have a daughter," he said.

Francine straightened up and threw the last of the sodden paper towels away. "Yes...Gretchen." Fear reached into her heart and plucked at the strings. What did he know about Gretchen?

For a long moment, his dark eyes held her. "How old is she? About three?"

She nodded, a barely perceptible head movement.

"She should have been mine, Frannie." Without a backward look, he turned and walked out the house.

She leaned against the wall and released a shuddery breath. Travis didn't know. Thank God, he didn't know that Gretchen was his daughter. And if Frannie had her wish, he would never know.

The puppy whined softly, breaking Francine's reverie. Travis was part of her past, as was this town...as were the unhappy memories of her life with her grandfather. She was only going to stay here long enough to get back on her feet, and then she would leave again. Comforted by this thought, Francine went back into the bedroom she now shared with her daughter.

As she crawled into bed, she was conscious of the sounds of insects serenading her outside the open window. The scent of honeysuckle drifted in on a warm breeze, and for a moment, Francine felt as if she'd been thrust back in time. She was ten years old again, sent here to live with her grandfather after the tragic accident that had taken her parents' lives. She felt alone, unhappy...and so frightened of what the future held. She knew only one thing for sure. Her future in no way included Travis Richards.

Travis slammed the back door closed, grabbed a beer from his own refrigerator and flopped down on a chair at his kitchen table. Damn Francine Webster.

He twisted off the top of the beer bottle and drank deeply, as if the tang of the liquid could erase the taste of bitterness that lingered in his mouth.

He'd often dreamed of Frannie returning to the small town of Cooperville, Nebraska. And always in his dreams she'd been dissipated and dissolute from her years in the city. He'd hoped she'd come back ugly so he would never want her again, but no, she was still just as stunning as she'd been five years ago, when she crawled out that window in the middle of the night and left him behind.

He closed his eyes, a vision of her filling his mind. Her hair was still a spill of dark satin down her back, her skin as soft-looking as smooth velvet. If there had been a change at all in her, it was in her eyes. The old defiance, the wild sparkle, was gone.

He finished his beer, threw the bottle away and

grabbed another. What he needed was to get good and drunk, banish the vision of her standing in front of him in that short, sexy pale blue nightshirt. Because the moment he saw her in that skimpy nightshirt, he'd remembered the sweet sensation of those sexy legs entwined with his, the taste of her breasts beneath the flick of his tongue, the feel of her rounded derriere cupped in his hands.

Damn her. He got up from the table and poured the last of his beer down the drain. He had a feeling that even if he was drunk, his memories of Frannie would haunt him.

He walked into his bedroom, not bothering to turn on the light. He slipped off his jeans and pulled his shirt over his head, then started for the bed. Instead, he found himself at the bedroom window...the window that faced Frannie's bedroom window.

How many times in those years of youth had he sat at this very window, watching hers for the flash of light that was their special signal? Once he saw the signal, he would leave his mother and sisters asleep and sneak out of the house to meet Frannie in the field of corn that had become their trysting place.

He frowned, trying to remember exactly when he'd realized he was in love with Frannie. The exact moment in time was impossible to pinpoint. It felt as if he'd been born loving her.

With a sigh of frustration, he yanked the curtains closed and flopped down on his bed. The Francine Webster he'd loved, the young girl he'd stood beside, fought for, dreamed with, was gone.

She was a woman now, a mother...with a history and life that didn't include him.

He hated her for that. He hated the fact that he wouldn't be her only lover, that within months of leaving him she'd found somebody else to love, somebody who had fathered her precious daughter.

Travis wondered why Frannie had come back here, back to the town she'd always hated and to the old man she'd insisted blamed her for her parents' death.

In the five years she was gone, there had been no phone calls, no letters, not a word from her. Apparently she had managed to erase him completely from her life.

Yet she had sent Poppy occasional postcards, little notes filled with her successes—a role in a Broadway play, a walk-on part in a soap opera. And although he and Poppy had never once spoken of her, Poppy always left the postcards in the center of the kitchen table, where Travis was sure to see them and keep track of her.

Travis drew a deep breath as he thought of the old man. He'd grown fond of Poppy. He and Poppy had developed a friendship that nourished them both, and Travis wasn't about to let Frannie's presence keep him away from Poppy. He also wasn't about to let Frannie touch any piece of his heart. Fate had given them one chance, and she'd run from it. Travis wasn't looking for second chances.

Chapter Two

Francine awoke slowly, vaguely aware of a sweet-scented morning breeze blowing across her and the distant sounds of voices. Gretchen was probably watching her cartoons, she told herself. Whoever had invented morning cartoons was a genius.

A dog barked, and a deep male voice rumbled a protest. Francine sat up, instantly remembering she wasn't in her little New York studio apartment, but back in Cooperville...back with Poppy.

She looked over at the cot where Gretchen had slept the night before. Empty. Panic surged. Where was Gretchen? Where was Beauty? And where was Poppy?

She jumped out of bed and yanked on a robe, then hurried out of the bedroom and into the kitchen. She stopped in the doorway, stunned by the scene that greeted her.

Poppy stood at the stove, his back to her as he

flipped pancakes. Beauty was tied just outside the back door, her nose pressed against the screen as she looked inside. A frown of concentration wrinkled Gretchen's forehead as she folded paper napkins to put at each of the three place settings at the table.

"I'm done, Poppy," she announced when she'd finished the task. "What can I do now?"

"Get the butter and milk out of the refrigerator, then you might go wake up your ma. Around here, if you want breakfast, you got to get up when it's served."

Francine tamped down old resentments at the gruffness in the old man's tone. "I'm awake." She stepped into the kitchen.

"Hi, Mommy. Poppy's making pancakes." Gretchen gave her a smile filled with sunshine and goodness, and instantly Francine's past hurts and resentments faded.

"Come here and give me a good-morning kiss," she said as she sank into a chair at the table.

Gretchen instantly complied, scrambling onto Francine's lap and wrapping her arms around her neck. Francine hugged her daughter close, reveling in the little-girl scent of innocence and sleepy warmth.

"Poppy says Beauty has to stay outside," Gretchen explained as she climbed off Francine's lap. "But he says he'll build her a doghouse."

"That's nice of him." Francine looked at her grandfather. His back was as rigid and unyielding as she remembered. "Is there anything I can do to help?" she asked.

He turned from the stove, a platter of pancakes in

hand. "It's all done. Coffee's on the stove, if you want a cup."

Poppy had never given in to the modern conveniences of automatic coffee machines when it came to brewing coffee. Rather than use a machine, he brewed it on top of the stove. And there was nothing like an old-fashioned freshly brewed cup of coffee. Francine poured herself a cup of the strong, steaming brew and sat back down at the table with her grandfather and daughter.

They filled their plates and ate for a few minutes in silence...the oppressive quiet Francine remembered from her years of growing up. A lifetime of meals shared between a grouchy old man and a sullen little girl. For Gretchen's sake, she attempted to break the pattern.

"How are things down at the diner?" she asked.

"Hard to keep good help." Poppy sipped his coffee, then poured syrup over a second pancake. "Business is always good, but nobody wants to be a waitress anymore."

"I could help out while I'm here," Francine offered after a moment's hesitation. It wasn't exactly the job of her dreams, but it was a job nevertheless and perhaps in a month or two she would make enough money to return to New York.

Poppy shrugged. "Suit yourself. I could use the help."

"I could work there, too," Gretchen put in. "Mommy and me used to eat at a diner in New York all the time."

"No, honey, if I work at the diner, we'll find a baby-sitter for you," Francine replied.

"She can stay here with me when you're at the diner," Poppy said. "I don't go in much anymore. I've got a manager that handles the day-to-day business."

Francine wanted to protest the arrangement. She didn't want Gretchen subjected to Poppy's cool indifference, the silences that had driven her away years ago. But she'd said that the main reason she'd come home was to give Poppy and Gretchen an opportunity to spend time together, to get to know each other, so how could she complain?

Besides, without paying a baby-sitter, she would be able to save her money and leave that much quicker. In any case, it would be interesting to see who fared better, the eternal, sunshine-smiling Gretchen, or the taciturn old man.

"Poppy, I can help you build Beauty's doghouse," Gretchen said. "And maybe we can paint it red. I think Beauty would like a red house."

Poppy snorted. "Don't need to paint a doghouse."

Gretchen looked at her grandfather soberly, then nodded in agreement. "You're right. Beauty will like a plain wood doghouse just as well."

Poppy stared at her for a long moment, then snorted once again. Within minutes, they'd finished eating. "Gretchen, go change out of your pajamas," Francine instructed her daughter as she began to clear the dishes from the table.

"You might want to take the girl down by the old chicken coop. I've got a rabbit hutch out there, with some new little ones," Poppy said when Gretchen had left the room.

"Her name is Gretchen," Francine replied tersely.

"I know that." He filled the sink with soapy water.

"Gretchen Marie Webster. The Marie is for Mama." She waited for him to say something, anything, but as usual he fell silent.

"I'll finish up here," he finally said, when there were only a few dishes left to dry and put away.

"Okay. I'll go change clothes and take Gretchen on a tour of the old homestead." She dried her hands on a dish towel, then left the kitchen and went upstairs to her bedroom.

Gretchen was there. Dressed in a pair of jeans and a pink T-shirt, she stood in front of the bulletin board, studying the remnants of Francine's past. "What's this, Mommy?" Gretchen pointed to a brown, withered clump of dried flowers.

"It used to be a corsage." Francine answered as she changed into jeans and a T-shirt.

"What's a corsage?" Gretchen asked curiously.

Francine brushed her long dark hair into a ponytail at the nape of her neck, then sat down on the cot next to her daughter. "A corsage is a little bouquet of flowers, usually given to a girl by her boyfriend."

"Did your boyfriend give this one to you?" Gretchen asked.

Francine touched the dried corsage, not surprised when the petals crumbled at her light contact. "Yes," she said, answering Gretchen's question. Oh, how easily the memory slipped into her mind of the night Travis had given her the flowers.

She was supposed to have been his date to the Sweetheart Ball, but Poppy had grounded her for some infraction of his rules. She'd spent the night in her room, crying over the missed opportunity, hating the old man who had been given the responsibility of raising her.

Near midnight, she'd seen the flashlight beam dancing on her wall, signaling her to escape out the window and meet Travis. There, in the middle of the cornfield, he'd greeted her. Clad in his best suit, he'd presented her with the corsage, then danced with her under the moonlight as the tinny sounds of his transistor provided their music.

"Did you have lots of boyfriends, Mama?" Gretchen's voice broke through Francine's memories. "I'll bet you did, 'cause you're so pretty."

Francine laughed and picked up Gretchen in her arms. "No. When I was little, I wasn't pretty at all. I was short and skinny and meaner than a cornered raccoon. Now, that's enough about me...how would you like to see some new baby bunnies?"

Gretchen's eyes opened wide. "Really?"

"Really." Francine laughed at her daughter's excitement. "Come on, let's go see what we can find outside."

Minutes later, Gretchen and Francine stepped out the back door and into the warm, sweet-scented sunshine. "We'll go down to the old chicken coop first," Francine said, pointing in the direction of a well-worn path.

As they walked, Francine steadfastly kept her gaze away from the neighboring house, not wanting to think about Travis. Instead, she focused on showing her daughter interesting parts of the farm.

"See that little building over there?" Francine asked, referring to the old smokehouse. "I used to play house in there when I was little."

"Do you think Poppy would let me play in there?" Gretchen asked.

"I don't know. We'll have to ask him." As they continued their journey down the path, Francine thought of those long summer days of her childhood.

The smokehouse had become her escape from the stern old man she'd been sent to live with while she grieved for the loving parents she'd lost. In the small confines of the old building, she would pretend she was on vacation with her parents, that she wasn't all alone.

It was in the smokehouse that she'd cried the tears she wouldn't let anyone else see. In the smokehouse, she'd dreamed of being famous, being loved. And it was in the smokehouse that she'd received her very first kiss...from Travis.

"Oh, Mommy, look!" Gretchen spied the chicken coop and, next to it, the rabbit hutch. She raced ahead, oohing and aahing at the furry little bunnies inside the mesh wiring.

Francine smiled as her daughter stood on tiptoe and stuck her fingers through the wire. "Aren't they cute?" Gretchen exclaimed.

"You want to hold one?"

"Can I?" Gretchen asked breathlessly.

Francine unlatched the gate and reached inside. She heard Gretchen's giggles as she tried to catch one, then another, of the little furry creatures. She finally managed to catch one and handed it to Gretchen, who sat down and placed it on her lap.

Francine smiled as she watched her daughter with the little baby animal. Gretchen seemed to have a special affinity for all things weak and frail, broken and helpless. Somehow, she collected hearts the way other little girls collected pretty ribbons.

As Gretchen petted and played with the bunny, Francine heard the whir of some sort of farm machinery as it approached them. She turned in the direction of the noise just in time to see a tractor cutting the weeds and brush around the old pond.

Travis sat on the tractor seat, like a king on a throne. He looked relaxed and proud at the same time. Shirtless beneath a pair of worn overalls, his shoulders looked lusciously tanned and wide beneath the thin denim straps.

His dark hair gleamed in the sunshine, although Frannie knew the sun would be unable to pull any highlights from the ebony thickness.

She averted her gaze from his direction, irritated that he hadn't grown fat or bald. Seeing him once again would have been much easier if he wasn't so devastatingly handsome.

"Come on, honey. We can come back to see the bunnies another time," Francine said, not wanting to see any more of Travis, not wanting to be pulled into old memories that only created bittersweet yearnings inside her. "We've got some unpacking to finish up."

"Bye-bye, little baby," Gretchen said to the bunny as her mother took it and put it back inside the hutch. "Who's that?" she asked, pointing to Travis, who raised a hand in greeting to the little girl.

"A neighbor."

"You think he'd give me a ride on his tractor?" Gretchen asked as she waved back to him.

"Tractors aren't for little girls. Come on, let's go." Francine led Gretchen back down the path, eager now to be inside, where she couldn't see Travis, and Travis wouldn't see them.

Funny how she hadn't realized how difficult it might be seeing him again. He's probably married, she told herself. Probably married to some sweet young woman whose biggest dream in the world was being a farmer's wife. For all she knew, he had a kid or two himself waiting for him at home.

Somehow that line of thought made it easier to deal with seeing him again. She'd like to think he was happy. She'd always wanted him to be happy. It made the choices she'd made feel right. Yet, at the same time, she hated him for finding that happiness without her.

It took most of the morning for Francine and Gretchen to unload the last of their belongings from the car and put everything away in the bedroom. They rearranged the bedroom in an effort to make more space. If they were going to stay, Francine would have moved into the spare bedroom. But, of course, they weren't going to be here for long.

It was just a few minutes before noon when they went back to the kitchen, where Poppy was once again standing in front of the stove.

"Hmm, something smells good," Gretchen said as she sniffed the tomato-and-garlic-laden air.

"Smells like Poppy's homemade spaghetti sauce," Frannie replied.

"Oh, I love spaghetti," Gretchen said.

"Poppy, you shouldn't have gone to all this trouble for lunch," Frannie said, oddly touched by the gesture of him making his special sauce for their first dinner at home.

"It's Tuesday. I always make sauce on Tuesdays," he replied. "Spaghetti on Tuesdays and meatball sandwiches on Wednesdays."

Oh, how quickly he could quell any positive feelings, Francine thought with a touch of bitterness. Heaven forbid he should allow her to think he'd gone to any trouble for her.

"Hey, Poppy, you've got too many plates on the table," Gretchen said.

"Nope, got four. There will be four of us for lunch." He turned off the burner beneath the boiling pasta and took the large pot to the sink to drain. "Travis eats lunch with me nearly every day."

Francine frowned. "Doesn't he have a wife to fix him lunch?"

"No wife," Poppy replied.

"Who is Travis?" Gretchen asked curiously.

"A neighbor," Francine answered.

"The one we saw on the tractor?" Francine nodded, and Gretchen smiled. "Oh, good, he looked nice."

He's not nice, Francine wanted to tell her daughter. He let me down and broke my heart. He was my best friend, my first love, and when I needed him most, he wasn't there for me.

Francine bit her bottom lip so that the words wouldn't escape. She didn't need Travis Richards.

"Poppy, I got to hold a baby bunny this morning," Gretchen told the old man. "It was so sweet and cute, and it wiggled its nose like this...." With the aid of her index finger, Gretchen wiggled her nose back and forth.

Poppy looked at the little girl as if she were a visitor from another planet. For just a moment, Francine could have sworn she saw a ghost of a smile lift the corners of his mouth.

The creak of the back door opening broke the moment, and Poppy turned back to the sink as Travis walked into the kitchen. "Hmm, Poppy, that smells great," he said as he nodded to Francine.

"Hi, I'm Gretchen." The little girl looked up at him with a friendly smile.

Travis got down on his haunches so that he was at eye level with her. Francine's stomach muscles tightened. Would he guess? Was it possible he might see characteristics of himself in the features of his daughter?

"Hello, Gretchen. It's nice to meet you. My name is Travis."

"I held a baby bunny!" Gretchen exclaimed.

"You did?" Travis stood, seeming to fill the kitchen with his overwhelming masculinity. "Maybe while you're here, your mother will bring you by my place. I've got a litter of new kittens."

"Kittens?" Gretchen clapped her hands together in excitement and looked at her mother. "Would you, Mommy?"

"We'll see," Francine replied, relaxing somewhat as Travis moved away from Gretchen and disappeared into the bathroom to wash his hands.

As Poppy put the food on the table, Francine motioned her daughter into a chair. "Anything I can do?" she asked.

"There's a salad in the refrigerator."

Francine retrieved the salad and placed it on the table as Travis reentered the room. Within minutes, they were all sitting down.

"I mowed all the weeds and brush away from the pond," Travis said to Poppy as he served himself a healthy portion of the spaghetti.

"Maybe you'll want to take the girl fishing," Poppy said to Francine.

"Oh, no, Mommy doesn't know how to fish," Gretchen quickly interjected. "I'd rather you take me fishing, Poppy. Grandpas know how to fish."

"How do you know so much about grandpas?" Poppy asked in his usual gruff tone.

"When Mommy told me we were coming here to see my grandpa, I asked all my friends at the day care about their grandpas, and they told me grandpas are nice...and cuddly. They can fish and fly a kite. They help you build stuff, and sometimes they have candy in their pockets."

Poppy snorted and shook his head.

Travis laughed, the deep sound stirring memories that ached inside Francine. "Sounds like you've got a lot to live up to, Poppy," Travis said.

Poppy snorted once again.

"How's your mother, Travis?" Francine asked.

He looked at her, his eyes dark and cool. "She passed away two years ago."

"Oh, I'm sorry. If I had known...I would have..."

"Sent flowers?"

Francine flushed, surprised by the anger that flashed in his eyes. What did he have to be angry about? *He* was the one who had let *her* down. He was the one who'd helped her build dreams, then refused to participate in making those dreams come true.

"How are your sisters?" she asked.

The anger in his eyes seemed to ebb slightly. "They're terrific. Margaret just left for her first year in college, and Susie got married three months ago."

"You must be very proud of them," she said.

"I am. They're pretty terrific." For just a moment, a smile curved the corners of his lips.

Francine wondered if he was remembering how his younger sisters had teased them unmercifully, following them whenever they were together, making smooching noises and singing about Travis and Francine up in a tree...*k-i-s-s-i-n-g*.   She and Travis had become quite adept at elaborate moves to lose the two, who loved to tease them.

She focused on her lunch, not wanting to remember those days and nights of childhood and adolescence. Those memories held such a curious mix of pleasure and pain.

"Hey, Travis, I've got a dog," Gretchen said, her mouth decorated with red sauce.

"Is that your dog that I saw tied outside?"

Gretchen nodded. "Her name is Beauty." She leaned toward Travis and lowered her voice to a conspiratorial tone. "She's not really a beauty, but we call her that to make her feel better."

"Ah, that's a smart thing to do," Travis replied.

The smile he gave Gretchen caused a visceral pull in Francine's stomach. When Gretchen was born, Francine hadn't dreamed that one day the little girl would sit next to her father at a kitchen table. She'd never dreamed Travis would be in their lives in any way, shape or form.

He's just a neighbor, she told herself. That was the way she needed to think of him. Just one of Poppy's neighbors. Besides, within a couple of months, she and Gretchen would be gone from here.

"We found Beauty in a garbage can," Gretchen explained to Travis. "Isn't that sad? Somebody tried to throw her away."

"I'd say she's one very lucky little puppy to have been found by you." Travis leaned over and wiped Gretchen's mouth with his napkin.

Again Francine felt overwhelmed by emotion. He would make a wonderful father. He'd always talked of the family he wanted. That had been his dream. "Gretchen, if you're finished eating, go wash your hands and face," Francine said, wanting to put some distance between father and daughter.

"Okay," she agreed easily. She got off her chair and started for the bathroom, then paused in the doorway. "Travis, do you like to fish?"

"Sure, it's one of my favorite things to do," he replied.

Gretchen smiled. "Then maybe when Poppy takes me fishing, you can go with us."

"That sounds like fun," Travis agreed. Gretchen skipped from the room, and Travis turned his gaze back to Francine. "She's a nice kid." He said it grudgingly, as if he'd have preferred her to be a spoiled brat. "She seems awfully smart for a three-year-old."

"She's very bright," Francine answered quickly. "Brighter than most her age."

"She talks too much," Poppy interjected.

Travis laughed. "Poppy, you'd think a mummy talks too much."

Again Francine could have sworn she saw the beginning of a smile cross Poppy's features. It disconcerted her, it was so out of character. She couldn't remember ever seeing Poppy smile.

"She looks just like you," Travis continued.

Francine nodded, at the moment grateful for that very fact. She held her breath, waiting for him to ask about Gretchen's father. To her relief, he resumed eating.

When they'd finished, Francine began to clear the table. "Just leave it. I'll take care of it," Poppy said. "You can walk Travis out and make sure that mutt has fresh water."

Reluctantly Francine followed Travis out the back door. In the distance, Gretchen sat on the ground, drawing pictures in the dirt for Beauty, who sat and watched, head cocked in doglike bewilderment.

Travis leaned against the porch railing, his gaze on the distant rows of corn and beans. "I've taken over all the farming of Poppy's fields. We split the profits and he makes me lunch every day."

"You don't owe me any explanations," she replied.

He turned and looked at her, his eyes once again holding a flicker of anger. "You're right. I don't owe you anything." He expelled a deep breath and raked a hand through his disheveled hair, his gaze going out into the distance. There was a moment of strained silence. "How long are you intending to stay?" he finally asked.

Francine shrugged. "I'm not sure. I'm kind of be-tween projects right now, so there's no reason to hurry back." She wasn't about to tell him that she'd been between projects for the past six months and couldn't afford to leave anytime soon. "Why?"

"It's nice that you brought your daughter to meet Poppy and spend time with him. He's not getting any younger, you know. But don't stay too long, Francine. Don't break his heart again." He didn't wait for her reply. He stepped off the porch and headed for the tractor parked in the distance.

Francine watched him go, shocked by his words. Don't break Poppy's heart? What a laugh. Poppy didn't have a heart to break.

As Travis passed Gretchen, he ruffled her hair and tweaked her nose. Gretchen's giggles floated on the breeze, and Francine made a mental note to go to the diner first thing in the morning. The sooner she could get some money together, the sooner she could get out of here. And this time, when she left, she'd never, ever look back.

Chapter Three

Francine left the farmhouse right after breakfast the next morning, after leaving careful instructions for Gretchen, who was staying home with Poppy.

She drove toward the diner, ten miles from the house and smack-dab in the center of the small town of Cooperville.

Rolling down the window, she breathed deeply of the air, enjoying the fragrance of rich black earth and fresh sunshine and tall grass. She'd missed these scents.

Shoulder-high corn waved tasseled tops in the early-August breeze. She could almost feel the tension of city living ebb with each field she passed.

She loved New York, with its frantic pace and perpetual motion. However, there had been times, deep in the heart of night, when sleep refused to come. Times when homesickness hit her and she longed for the familiar creak of Poppy's rocking chair, the smell of hay being cut and baled, the particular hue of blue sky found only in Nebraska.

And if she dug deep enough into her soul, she'd have to admit, albeit painfully, that she had missed Travis. There had been a time when they were able to finish each other's sentences, so attuned to each other they were. Two misfits who never quite fit in with their peers, who always seemed a step behind or a step ahead of everyone else, but in perfect rhythm with each other.

She'd broken that harmony by leaving. He'd destroyed any remnant by so easily letting her go. She tightened her grip on the steering wheel, fighting a combination of regret and resentment.

With relief, she turned into the parking lot of Della's Diner. Della had been Francine's grandmother, but she'd passed away when Francine was a baby. Poppy hadn't changed the name of the diner, despite the absence of the woman, whom Francine couldn't even remember.

She found an empty spot in the nearly full lot and parked. Instead of getting out of the car immediately, she sat for a few moments and eyed the place that was as much a home to her as the two-story farmhouse.

Although weathered, with faded and peeling paint covering the outside, the diner held a certain quaint charm. Pink striped awnings protected the two front windows from the morning sun, and large urns on either side of the front door offered a plethora of petunias and impatiens in various sizes and colors.

Poppy owned the diner, but he'd never worked it full-time. Still, when Francine was young, she'd spent

many hours here. She'd worked after school, prefer-
ring the chaotic atmosphere of the diner to the loneliness of the house.

It had been waitressing tip money, squirreled away
through high school, that allowed her to leave Cooperville five years ago. It seemed ironic that once
again she was depending on the diner to help fulfill
her dream to get back to New York.

She got out of the car and headed inside. A cowbell
jangled as she opened the door, and immediately she
was greeted by rich home-cooking smells and the
noise inherent in a busy diner.

Betty Jean Prather, the big-boned manager, with
hair dyed the color of flames, saw her come in and
made a beeline toward her, her ample arms open wide
in greeting. "Well, if it isn't our own little star, come
home to visit." She wrapped Francine in a welcoming
full-body hug, her apron emanating familiar scents of
hot grease, sliced onions, rose perfume and mint gum.

Francine returned her hug. Betty Jean had been the
only female influence in Francine's life. It was Betty
Jean who had taken Francine to buy her first bra,
Betty Jean who'd told her the facts of life.

"Let me take a look at you." Betty Jean released
Francine and stepped back, her blue eyes gazing at
Francine critically. "You don't look like the big city
hurt you none," she observed, then grinned. "I saw
you on that soap opera, honey. Goodness me, that was
the most exciting thing in my life. I called all my
friends and relatives to tell them my little Francine
was on the tube. She's a big star, I told them all."

Francine slid on to a stool at the counter, fighting
off a wave of guilt and pride. Guilt because Betty was

obviously so impressed and seemed to believe Francine had "made it" in the world of acting. "It was a lot of fun. I was disappointed I got killed off within three days."

Betty Jean grinned. "But you died such a fine death." She hustled around the counter. "Let me get you a cup of coffee. Poppy called me this morning to tell me you'd be coming in to work while you're home visiting." She splashed coffee into a cup, then shoved it in front of Francine. "We can definitely use your help. Breakfast is pretty manageable, but we get a big lunch rush, and my best waitress quit last week."

"I can work whenever you need me," Francine replied.

"Weekends I could use you for both the lunch and dinner rushes."

"Fine," Francine agreed.

"Oops, hang tight." Betty went to the window that separated the dining area from the kitchen and grabbed two plates of steaming food. As she delivered the orders, Francine looked around the room, recognizing several people, and smiling in greeting.

"I heard you've got a little girl," Betty said as she returned.

Francine smiled and nodded. "Her name is Gretchen."

Betty grinned wryly. "Some slick city boy must have sweet-talked you good." Betty shook her head. "I always thought you and Travis would end up married and with a dozen children."

Francine's chest tightened at the mention of his name. "I was surprised to learn he hasn't married."

"It's not from lack of opportunity. Travis is the most eligible bachelor in town, and most young women and half their mothers have tried to light a fire in that man." Betty leaned closer. "But I think when you left Cooperville, you took all the fire right out of him." As more orders came up, Betty left to distribute them.

Francine stared down into her coffee, Betty's words ringing in her ears, echoing in her heart. He could have come with her. He could have stopped her. He'd done neither.

The past. It was all the past, and there was no way to go back and change it, fix it or forget it. She just had to live with it.

"Betty, fill me out a time card," she said, then drained her coffee cup and stood. "I'm ready to get to work."

The morning passed quickly as Francine kept herself busy waiting on tables, cashing out customers and carrying dirty dishes back to the kitchen.

She was embarrassed by the number of people who came in and mentioned seeing her brief stint on the soap opera, assuming she was a big star home for a vacation and working only to help out her grandfather.

It surprised her that apparently the brief postcards she sent Poppy, filled with exaggerated successes, had been shared with many of the regular customers of the diner. Her little white lies were coming back to haunt her.

"Hey, Francine." A man at a table in the back of the diner waved her over. He'd come in with the lunch rush and been served by Betty.

"Can I get you something?" she asked, wishing nothing more than a moment to take off her shoes and rub her aching feet. She'd forgotten how physically demanding waitressing could be.

He held out his hand. "Barry Simmons. I'm the editor of the *Cooperville Press*."

"Nice to meet you, Mr. Simmons." She shook his hand. He was an attractive man, with sandy hair and warm brown eyes. She guessed him to be in his late twenties or early thirties. "What can I do for you?" she asked.

"Let me do a story on you. You know, local girl makes good."

"Oh, please, no." Francine shook her head.

"It would make a great human-interest story," Barry returned.

"Mr. Simmons, I'm home on vacation. The last thing I want is some story about me in the local paper." Francine drew in a deep breath. "Besides, I'm not exactly a household name. In fact, like most actresses in New York, I'm barely surviving."

Barry's smile was open and genuine. "The way Betty Jean talks about you, I figured you might be up for a couple of Academy Awards, or at least an Emmy or two."

Francine laughed. "I was in a soap opera for three days and an off-Broadway play that ran for six weeks. I was an extra for one episode of a television drama, and that's about the extent of my career so far." She smiled ruefully. "Not exactly fodder for a local-girl-makes-good article, although enough to tickle the people in this small town."

"I appreciate your honesty, Francine." His smile

warmed. "Okay, if I can't write a story, perhaps you'll let me buy you dinner before you return to New York."

Francine's cheeks warmed. She couldn't remember the last time anyone had asked her out. "I'm not sure what my schedule is going to be like," she said, hedging. "Between working here and taking care of my daughter, I'll probably be pretty busy. Besides, I really don't date much."

Barry shrugged, his friendly smile still intact. "Can't blame a guy for trying."

Francine smiled, glad he hadn't taken her brush-off too personally. "It was nice meeting you, Barry. Now I've got to get back to work before Betty Jean accuses me of loafing."

A few minutes later, as Francine cleared a table, Betty grabbed her by the arm. "Why didn't you take Barry up on his offer of dinner?" she asked.

Francine laughed. "Betty Jean, I swear you have ears in the back of your head. How did you know he asked me out?"

Betty grinned. "He told me he was going to when I took his order, and he told me you turned him down when he left. Why didn't you go out with him? He's a nice guy. The other good catch in town."

"I'm not looking for a good catch," Francine replied. "Besides, the stupidest thing I could do would be to get involved with somebody here, when I intend to leave in a month or two and return to New York."

"I didn't say you had to sleep with him, honey, just have dinner with him," Betty teased.

Francine shook her head. "I'm just not into relationships right now." What she refused to tell Betty was that she hadn't been interested in a relationship since the night she left Cooperville.

Something had broken inside her when Travis so easily allowed her to walk out of his life...and she knew that something had been her heart.

Travis sat on the porch, a beer in his hand, as he watched Poppy and Gretchen work on a doghouse for Beauty. The late-afternoon sun slanted deep shadows across the lawn, and the air smelled of honeysuckle and fresh-cut grass.

He took a sip of the icy beer, his gaze focused on Francine's daughter. The child was the spitting image of her mother, from the long dark hair and blue eyes to the dimple that danced in her left cheek. Watching her grow up would be like watching Francine all over again.

There was no indication of what her father might look like, no genetic stamp from him at all on the little girl's features.

Travis tightened his grip on the neck of the beer bottle, not wanting to think of the man who'd held Francine in his arms, made love to her...made a baby with her.

Travis and Francine had spent many nights talking about their dreams for the future, hers of stardom and fame, and his of home and family. Despite their differences, Travis had never doubted that they would somehow be bound together for all eternity.

He'd never believed she would walk away from him and never look back. He'd certainly never considered that mere months after leaving him, she would run into the arms of another man.

He wanted to dislike the kid...the fruit of Francine's betrayal...but it was impossible. She was a charmer, with the disposition of a sunny day. And despite the fact that she looked like her mother, she didn't share the personality that Francine had possessed as a child.

Francine had spent most of her youth being mad...mad at fate for taking her parents, mad at Poppy for not giving her what she needed, mad at the world for being dealt a bad hand.

He hoped New York and her success had eased some of that anger, that she'd found the kind of happiness he and Cooperville apparently couldn't give her. It seemed only right that one of them should be happy.

Draining the bottle of its last sip, he stood and walked over to where Gretchen and Poppy were working. "Looks like it's going to be a fine doghouse," he observed.

Gretchen smiled up at him. "I knew Poppy would make the bestest doghouse in the world. He's the bestest grandpa in the whole world."

"And I think you might just be a little girl who's full of beans," Poppy returned.

Gretchen giggled. "What kind of beans, Poppy?"

Poppy set the hammer down and eyed her intently. "I'm thinking that today you're probably full of kidney beans."

Gretchen giggled again, and a smile swept over Poppy's face. Almost immediately, he cleared his throat, picked up the hammer and went back to work.

Travis fought a wave of amusement. Gretchen would be good for the crusty old man. In the past five years, Travis had gotten very close to Poppy and he knew he hid a heart of gold beneath his grouchy facade.

He also knew that Poppy's life had been pretty empty. Travis hoped Gretchen could fill that emptiness, at least for a little while.

A cloud of dust swirled in the distance and signaled the approach of a car. "It's Mommy!" Gretchen exclaimed as the car pulled into the driveway.

Francine parked and got out of the car, her attention focused solely on her daughter, who danced out to greet her. Clad in a pink-and-white striped uniform from the diner, Francine looked worn, hot and tired.

As Gretchen took her mother's hand and led her over to the half-finished doghouse, Travis slipped inside the house and grabbed a beer from the refrigerator.

When he returned to the porch, Francine sat on the steps, her back against the handrail post as she watched the two carpenters nearby.

"Here." He held out the beer.

"Thanks." She took the cold bottle from him and held it to her forehead. "There are several things I'd forgotten about being here."

"Like?" He sat down next to her.

"For one thing, how hot it gets in August."

She leaned her head back and placed the bottle against her neck, the action strangely erotic. A flicker of desire stirred in Travis, both surprising and irritating him. Back and forth she rubbed the bottle against the hollow of her throat, as if finding the coolness of the bottle eminently pleasing.

Travis watched, half hypnotized by the movement.

Stifling a groan, he grabbed the bottle from her and twisted off the top, then gave it back to her.

She took a deep sip. "Oh, that tastes wonderful. I'd forgotten how good a cold beer can taste on a hot summer day." She kicked off her shoes and scrunched her toes. "The other thing I'd forgotten is how hard it is to be up on your feet all day waiting on people."

"You've just grown soft with your new life-style as a successful actress."

Her eyes flashed at him, and she opened her mouth as if to speak, but instead looked back at Poppy and Gretchen.

Travis stretched his legs out before him. "Won't be long before fall will be here and I won't have a minute for any soft living. The corn will have to be picked, and all the machinery cleaned and winterized."

"You sound just like a farmer."

He looked at her intently. "I am a farmer, and that's what I'll always be, just a simple farmer."

For a moment, their gazes remained locked. In her eyes he saw unspoken recriminations, but he refused to feel guilty.

He knew her dream had been that they both would go to New York and find work on the stage, but that had never been part of his dream.

She sighed and looked away. "How long have they been at it?" She gestured toward Poppy and Gretchen.

He shrugged. "Most of the day. Poppy could have built three doghouses in the time they've spent, but he's letting Gretchen do most of the work, so it's taking a long time."

She smiled and shook her head, her dark hair waving silkily with the movement. "Poppy showing patience—who would have believed it?" she said ruefully.

"It's been five years, Francine. People change." He clenched his hands, fighting the impulse to reach out and touch her hair, twirl its softness around his fingers.

It irritated him that despite the fact that she'd walked away from him, in spite of the fact that she'd taken his heart and cast it aside, he still wanted her.

"Poppy hasn't changed," she told him. "It's just impossible to be hateful to Gretchen. She refuses to see meanness in anyone." She took another long draw of her beer.

Travis knew just how her mouth would taste, like heated honey with the tang of the cold beer. He could remember in vivid detail the softness of her skin, the heat of her body as it had moved against his own. Again anger swept through him, anger directed at himself, focused on her.

"Where's her father?" he asked, knowing it was a topic that would keep his anger alive, usurping the more dangerous emotion of desire.

He felt her stiffen, the tension that instantly filled her body. "He's no longer a part of our lives."

Travis wondered if she'd loved him desperately, or if those first few months of loneliness in a strange city had driven her into his arms. In any case, he supposed, it didn't matter. "That's too bad," he replied. "Having lost my dad when I was so young, I know the space such a loss leaves behind."

"Gretchen is fine," she said defensively. "She's perfectly well-adjusted. I'm all she needs. I love her enough for two parents."

"Whoa." Travis held up his hands in supplication. "You don't have to prove anything to me."

Her gaze slid away from him, back to her daughter. "She's never even asked about her father. At the day care she goes to most of the children are from single-parent families. If and when she questions me about him, I'll be honest with her. In the meantime, it's not an issue." There was a note of finality in her voice.

"Mommy, look!" Gretchen stood next to the completed doghouse, her face beaming with pride. "It's done!"

"It looks wonderful, honey," Francine answered.

As Gretchen placed Beauty on a leash and introduced the dog to her new home, Poppy joined Travis and Francine on the porch.

"Did Betty Jean give you a hard time today?" he asked as he eased himself on to the porch swing.

"No more than she ever did," Francine answered. "I'll say one thing, that woman has more energy than three people half her age."

"She's a good manager, keeps everything running smoothly for me."

"She's also the biggest gossip in town," Travis said dryly.

Francine laughed, the melodic sound once again stirring embers of desire inside Travis. "You're absolutely right about that. Within fifteen minutes of working with her, I knew everything that happened to everyone since I left town.''

Travis stood, suddenly needing to get some distance from her. Her laugh, her scent, the press of her breasts against the bodice of the uniform...all of it conspired to make him want her. And he didn't want to want her.

''I've got to get home,'' he said as he stepped off the porch.

''You're welcome to stay for supper,'' Poppy offered.

Travis shook his head. ''No thanks. I've got things to do at home.''

''Bye, Travis!'' Gretchen yelled as he strode toward his pickup.

He waved at the little girl, then climbed into the truck and started the engine. As he drove down the lane that connected Poppy's land to his own, he tightened his grip on the steering wheel, trying to analyze why, after all this time, after all his hurt and anger, he still wanted Francine.

Perhaps it was because evening was falling. That had always been the time of day when, years ago, he'd begin to anticipate being with her. At that time, always as the sun began to lower in the west, his heart would begin the quickened pace of excitement.

No matter how tired he was from hours in school, then more hours in the fields, he'd never been too tired to meet Francine. As shadows deepened into purple twilight, he'd always gotten a new burst of energy, sparked by the knowledge that after dark Francine would sneak out of her house and they'd spend time together.

Sometimes they would meet and just sit side by side, not needing to speak or touch, but comforted by each other's presence. Other times they'd kissed, caressed, barely calling a halt before getting completely out of control. He would go home, so inflamed by their teasing that sleep wasn't possible for hours.

Somehow, he'd always assumed that when he finally made love to Francine it would be in a big, soft bed, when he finally made her his wife. But that hadn't happened. The last night they shared, when they finally made love, it had been an act born from love and desperation. A final memory that would both haunt him and warm him forever.

Memories, that was all he was feeling. Just the memory of desire, the retention of pleasant times imprinted on his brain.

He eased his grip on the steering wheel, relieved by the rationalization. Of course that was all it was. For just a moment, he'd gotten caught up in the memory of loving Francine, but that had nothing to do with the here and now, with reality.

He'd be less than human if he didn't feel some emotion left over from the closeness of their shared past. And he would be more the fool if he allowed himself to believe that his heart felt anything for her except a fondness bred in simple memory.

Chapter Four

"See you tomorrow," Francine said to Betty Jean as she started out the door of the diner.

As she walked to her car, she patted her pocket, where her tips for the day rested against her heart. She'd been working at the diner for a week, and between what she had in her pocket and her cache of tip money in the drawer in her bedroom, she had a little over three hundred dollars. Not bad, she thought, congratulating herself.

Thank goodness the diner did a brisk business and most of the people were generous when it came to tips. What surprised Francine more than anything was that she enjoyed the work, liked the social interplay with the customers and the physical activity that made her too tired for dreams at night.

What also surprised Francine was the fact that Poppy and Gretchen seemed to be getting along just fine. Twice Poppy had taken the little girl fishing, and he'd put Gretchen in charge of feeding and watering the bunnies, a chore she adored.

On the one hand, Francine was grateful that the arrangement of Poppy watching Gretchen while she was at work was working so well. On the other hand, she couldn't help but resent the fact that somehow Poppy managed to lose part of his grouchy nature whenever he was around Gretchen.

There was the memory of a little girl who'd never managed to make Poppy love her inside Francine. And she resented the fact that Poppy was able to give to her child what he'd never been able to give to her.

She rolled down the window, her thoughts going from Poppy to Travis. Thankfully, with her schedule at the diner, she'd seen very little of him in the past week. Twice he'd come over in the evening, but he and Poppy had sat on the porch to visit and Francine had remained in the house.

She'd thought her heart would stop when he asked her about Gretchen's father. Guilt had swept through her as she dodged his questions. She realized she should have told him years ago that their single night of passion had not been without results. However, at the time, she'd thought her reasons for not telling him were sound ones.

She wasn't about to remain in Cooperville so that he could play the role of father. Certainly, if he'd wanted her to stay, wanted a future with her, he would have asked her to stay and build a life with him on that last night, when they made love.

Besides, Travis had been inundated with responsibility, caring for his sick mother and his younger sisters. He hadn't needed one more responsibility. And now it no longer mattered. Too much time had passed for her to uncover the secret now. Besides, the truth would only complicate everyone's lives.

Frannie shoved these thoughts aside as she pulled into the driveway that led to the farmhouse. She couldn't change things with Travis, and as far as Poppy was concerned, she shouldn't look a gift horse in the mouth. She was grateful that he was being kind to Gretchen, and Gretchen seemed to thrive on her time with her great-grandfather.

She parked in front of the house, a sense of home-coming filling her heart when she saw Poppy and Gretchen sitting on the front porch waiting for her.

"Hi, Mommy." Gretchen bounded down the steps and flew into Francine's arms.

"Hi, pumpkin," Francine returned, hugging her daughter tight. "Did you have a good day?" she asked as she carried the little girl to the porch.

"We had a great day," Gretchen replied. "We caught two big catfish, and I saw a snake, and look—" She pointed to Beauty's doghouse, now a fire-engine red. "We just finished it. Isn't it beauti-ful?"

"It's gorgeous." Francine looked at Poppy. His face was flushed from the heat, and his wrinkles ap-peared deeper than usual. He sported a red splash of paint on one cheek. "You look tired," she observed.

"I am."

"I thought you weren't going to paint it."

He frowned. "Little Miss Beans was going to nag me to death. That mutt had to have a red house."

Gretchen beamed and sat down next to Poppy on

the swing. "What kind of beans am I full of today?" she asked.

It had become a game between the two of them, and as Francine watched Poppy pretend to think before answering, her heart swelled.

"I'm thinking you're probably filled with baked beans today," he answered, and Gretchen giggled as if he were the smartest, wittiest man she'd ever known. A spark of something akin to affection lit the old man's eyes, and again Francine felt a bittersweet ache inside.

"I'd better get in and start supper," she said, eager to get out of her uniform and into something cooler and more comfortable.

In her bedroom, she tucked the tip money in the top bureau drawer, then changed into a shiftlike sleeveless sundress. She pulled her long hair into a ponytail, grateful to get the heavy length off her neck, then went out into the kitchen to fix the evening meal.

They had just finished eating an hour later when Travis appeared at the back door. "I could smell that coffee clear over at my house," he said, gesturing toward the glass pot perking on the stovetop.

"There's a cup that's got your name on it," Poppy said as he pushed his empty plate aside.

"Why don't you both take your coffee out on the porch and I'll clean up the dishes?" Francine suggested. She didn't want Travis in the kitchen, where she could smell his freshly showered scent and feel his dark gaze on her. He disturbed her in a way that was far too pleasant for comfort.

"Sounds good to me," Poppy said, and got up from the table.

"Travis, we painted Beauty's house today," Gretchen said. She grabbed Travis's hand. "Come see how pretty it looks."

"Go on and let her show you," Poppy said to Travis. "I'll carry out the coffee."

As Travis and Gretchen disappeared out the door, Francine busied herself clearing up the dishes. She and Poppy had made an agreement to take turns with the cooking and cleaning up of the evening meals. Tonight was her turn.

"That man should have himself some kids," Poppy said.

Francine gazed at him sharply, wondering if he was trying to let her know he knew her secret. He stood at the doorway, looking out at Travis and Gretchen, and Francine realized it was just a passing comment made in innocence.

"According to Betty Jean, half the women in town would love to accommodate him," Francine replied.

"Maybe, but he doesn't seem to be interested in any of them." He left the doorway and poured the two cups of coffee. "Why don't you get yourself a cup and sit with us when you're done in here?"

Francine looked at him in surprise. "Maybe I will for a few minutes," she agreed.

He nodded, then disappeared out the door. Francine stared after him, shocked by his indication that he might want her company.

Travis had indicated that it was possible Poppy had changed in the past five years. Francine had dismissed the very thought. For her, whatever he offered would be too little, too late. Or was it?

She finished the dishes in record time, then carried

a cup of coffee out onto the porch, where Poppy sat in the swing and Travis sprawled in a lounge chair. Gretchen was playing with Beauty, trying to teach the pup how to fetch a stick.

Francine sank down on the top step of the porch and leaned her head against the railing. It was a beautiful evening. A refreshing breeze had kicked up, diffusing some of the heat of the day and bringing with it the scents of blooming flowers, sweet clover and fresh sunshine.

Gretchen, apparently tired of fetching the stick herself, joined Francine on the step. "Hey, poppet." Francine smoothed a strand of dark hair away from her daughter's eyes.

"Mommy, will you play a game with me?"

"What kind of a game?" Francine asked.

"I don't know." Gretchen frowned thoughtfully. "Something fun." Her face lit with an idea. "I know...why don't we all play a game of hide-and-seek?"

"Oh, honey, I don't think anyone wants to play hide-and-seek," Francine replied.

"But it will be so much fun. Please?" Gretchen wheedled.

Poppy set his mug down next to him. "I suppose I could rustle up enough energy for a little hide-and-seek."

Gretchen jumped up and threw her arms around the old man. "Oh, Poppy, I knew you were the bestest grandpa in the whole wide world!" she exclaimed.

Poppy frowned and cleared his throat. "You'll just nag us all to death until we play."

Travis stood, an easy grin on his face. "I have to

warn you, Gretchen. I'm the best in the world at hiding. Years ago, when your mom and I used to play hide-and-seek, it would take her hours and hours to find me."

Gretchen's eyes widened. "You and Mom used to play hide-and-seek?"

Travis nodded, his gaze lingering on Francine, and in his eyes she saw memories of those carefree childhood days. Francine returned his smile, for the moment allowing herself the sheer pleasure of those pleasant memories.

"If I remember correctly, I wasn't exactly a slouch when it came to finding good hiding places," she returned.

"Oh, this is going to be so much fun." Gretchen jumped up and down and clapped her hands together with excitement. "Okay. I'll be it, and I'll count to one hundred, and you guys hide."

She ran over by the big tree in the yard, squeezed her eyes closed, then began to count as the adults scrambled off the porch in search of hiding places. As Poppy headed toward the barn, Francine looked around for the perfect place to hide. A nearby oak tree beckoned, but Francine feared that would be the first place her daughter would look.

Instead she headed for the cornfield, knowing the shoulder-high stalks would make a terrific hiding place. As she ran through the narrow rows, deep enough to be hidden from Gretchen's view, she heard her daughter stumbling over numbers as she reached the forties.

"Forty-two. Forty-eight. Fifty..." Gretchen called,

and Francine made a mental note to go over those numbers with her daughter.

"Great minds think alike."

She jumped as Travis appeared next to her, a piece of corn silk decorating the top of his head. She grinned and picked the silky strand off him. "Get lost, buster. I was here first."

"It's a big field—surely there's room for both of us."

However, as he moved closer to her, she felt as if the field had shrunk, become far too small for both of them. He stood so close to her she could smell him, the scent of warm sunshine and minty soap and the subtle hint of spicy cologne.

She wanted to move, find another place to hide, a place where she wouldn't be able to smell the evocative scent of him.

"Ready or not...here I come!" Gretchen yelled from behind the tree, and Francine knew that if she moved now, Gretchen would see the telltale waving of the cornstalks. Instead, she crouched down, making certain her head couldn't be seen above the corn.

Travis did the same, stooping down so close to her she could feel the heat from his body. Francine sat on the ground, attempting to gain some sort of distance from him. She frowned as Travis sat next to her, his thigh pressed intimately against her.

"Remember the night we hid here in the cornfield while Poppy cussed and stormed about your grades?" Travis asked.

Despite her discomfort at his nearness, she couldn't help but smile at the memory. "Oh, you remember how angry he was? I thought he'd catch me and tan my hide for sure."

"He knew you were smart enough to get better grades than you did," Travis observed, his gaze warm on her.

"I was," she agreed easily.

He leaned closer to her, his breath warm on her face. "That was the first and only time I ever saw you cry." With his fingertip, he touched her cheek in a soft, featherlike caress. "Big fat tears raced down your face, and I wanted to yell at Poppy for upsetting you so much."

Francine's heartbeat quickened, and her mouth grew dry. She knew she should scoot away from Travis, not allow him to touch her with such a sweet intimacy. But she couldn't. She felt frozen in place, captive to his nearness.

"You were so afraid Poppy was going to send you away. You cried in my arms for hours."

Francine gave a slight nod, wishing he would remove his hand from her face and fighting the need to lean into his touch. "I thought I'd finally pushed him too far." Francine closed her eyes, remembering the emotions that had swept through her as she anticipated Poppy's rage.

That had been the moment when she realized that although she hated living here with Poppy, the thought of living anywhere else was more horrifying. It had also been the moment when she truly believed that if she had to live without Travis, she might die. She now knew that wasn't true.

"Francine." His voice was soft, and when she opened her eyes, she knew he was going to kiss her.

She also knew she should stop him, but heaven help her, she wanted it.

His lips touched hers, tentative at first, but filled with heat. Sparks ignited inside Francine, and she opened her mouth to him, wanting him to deepen the kiss. He did, placing a hand behind her head as his mouth explored hers with an intimacy that stole her breath away.

Sweet, familiar sensations burst through her, half-forgotten feelings of want and need. She had spent the past five years trying to forget the heat of his kisses, the fire in his touch, and in a solitary kiss, he'd brought it all back. All the memories of that single night they'd made love flooded through her.

His hand worked to draw off the band that held her hair captive. When he succeeded, it spilled down her back and he tangled his hand in it.

"Poppy, I found you!" Gretchen's delighted giggles penetrated through the fog Travis's kiss had created, and Francine jerked away from him.

She saw the desire, dark and rich, in his eyes, just as it had been so many years ago. It frightened her that desire remained between them, despite the distance of time and space. But it hadn't been enough five years ago, and it certainly wasn't enough now.

"Ally, ally out in free!" Gretchen yelled.

"You shouldn't have done that," Francine said softly as she reached up and touched her lips.

His eyes flickered, dark and fathomless. "I know." Then he stood and ran toward the porch where Gretchen and Poppy awaited.

Francine remained for a long moment, waiting for her heart to stop pumping so fast and her breathing to return to normal. She spied her hair tie on the ground and quickly pulled her hair back into an untidy ponytail.

When she finally felt as if she'd regained her equilibrium, she stood and walked slowly back to where the others waited for her.

They played three more games of hide-and-seek, Francine choosing her hiding places carefully, so that she wouldn't end up in the same place as Travis. By the time they finished the last game, darkness had fallen, making any further play impossible.

"Time for a bath and bed," Francine said to Gretchen.

"Yeah, and it's time for me to get back to my place," Travis said.

"Goodbye, Travis," Gretchen said, and tugged him down so that she could give him a kiss on the cheek. "We'll play again, and next time I'll find you no matter where you hide."

He laughed and touched the end of her nose in obvious affection. "Goodbye, sweetheart. You sleep tight and don't let the bugs bite." Gretchen giggled. Travis straightened and looked at Francine. "Sweet dreams, Frannie."

She nodded and he walked out and got into his pickup. Frannie. Nobody but Poppy and Travis had ever called her that. She watched his truck lights all the way to his house and remained on the porch until he had gone inside and a light blinked on in his living room.

Was he thinking of her? Of their kiss? Why, oh, why, had he kissed her? And why had she let him? She turned and went into the house, where Poppy had disappeared into his bedroom and Gretchen was getting ready for her bath.

An hour later, she tucked a sweet-smelling, clean Gretchen into bed. She sat on the edge of the cot and stroked Gretchen's forehead. "Good night, sweetheart," she said.

Gretchen smiled, her eyelids at half-mast. "It was fun playing hide-and-seek, wasn't it, Mommy?"

"Lots of fun," Francine answered.

"Can we stay here forever, Mommy? I like it here. I like Poppy and Uncle Travis..."

"Uncle Travis?"

A dimple danced in Gretchen's cheek. "I decided to pretend he's my uncle. I like him bunches."

"Don't you miss New York and all your friends at the day care?"

Gretchen frowned thoughtfully. "Yeah, I miss them. But I like it here better than New York."

Francine leaned down and gave her a kiss. "Go to sleep now. It's late, and we can talk more tomorrow."

Gretchen nodded and closed her eyes. Francine left the room, disturbed by the conversation. She didn't want Gretchen to like it here. That would only complicate matters.

She walked back out onto the porch, where night had stolen the last of the day. Sitting down on the swing, she touched her fingers to her lips as she remembered the kiss she'd shared with Travis. She couldn't allow that to happen again. She absolutely refused to let her heart be touched by Travis. More than ever, she realized how important it was for her to get some money together and leave...leave before her heart could get broken once again.

* * *

Travis jumped up from the sofa to grab the ringing telephone. "Hello?"

"Ah, you're home. I tried earlier, and nobody answered." Susie's voice filled him with a sense of pleasure.

"I was over at Poppy's," Travis explained. He carried the phone with him to the sofa and sat back down.

"Oh, yeah, I heard Francine was back in town."

"She is."

"So?"

Travis heard the anticipation in his sister's voice. "So what?" he asked irritably. Since his sister's recent marriage, she seemed to have appointed herself Travis's personal matchmaker.

"So...have you seen her? Any sparks left between the two of you?"

Sparks? Hell, he'd felt a brushfire sweep through him when he kissed Francine. But he wasn't about to admit that to anyone...especially to his well-meaning but nosy younger sister. "Susie, that's all in the past. Francine and I were just crazy kids."

Susie's sigh was audible across the phone line. "I just thought... I hoped..."

"Yeah, well, don't," Travis interjected. "Francine's just here for a short vacation. She's got a career that's going places. She has all of New York City at her fingertips. I'm sure the city is filled with all kinds of witty, wonderful men who can take her to fancy restaurants and Broadway plays. She certainly has no interest in a simple farmer." For some reason, the thought of those city men with Francine made his stomach ache.

"Travis, to me you'll always be more than a simple farmer," Susie chided him softly. "To me you'll always be a hero."

He smiled, a burst of warmth spreading through him at his sister's words. He'd certainly never considered himself anything like a hero. He'd just been a man taking care of business, doing what was best for his family and the people he loved.

However, one thing was clear: He would be nothing short of a fool if he ever forgot that he was just a simple man, a farmer, content with the uncomplicated elements of his life.

That hadn't been enough for Francine five years ago...and it certainly wouldn't be enough for her now.

Chapter Five

Francine swiped the counter with a clean sponge and checked her watch. Nine-thirty. Another thirty minutes and she could put the Closed sign on the diner door and go home.

Betty had gone home twenty minutes earlier, declaring the place too dead to warrant both of them staying to close. The diner had been slow all night, and Betty had explained to Francine that it was a typical Wednesday night.

With the counters and tables all clean, and nothing left to do, Francine poured herself a cup of coffee and sat on a stool at the end of the counter.

From the kitchen, she could hear the sounds of Benny Walton, the cook, cleaning up. He'd shut down the grill moments ago and told her anyone who came in this late could order nothing but the desserts that were already made and drinks. For all intents and purposes, the kitchen was closed.

She sipped her coffee slowly, finding it difficult to believe she'd been home for almost two weeks. Between her work at the diner and spending time with Gretchen, the days passed so quickly it was almost frightening.

Some of her old high school classmates had come into the diner, surprising Francine with their friendliness. Apparently, in their eyes, Francine had made it big, and they all spoke of her soap-opera stint with a curious blend of awe and envy.

It was odd for Francine, who could still remember many of their cruel taunts. "Toothpick legs." "Skinny orphan." Francine, more than anyone, knew how cruel children could be to each other, and she'd been chosen the sacrificial scapegoat by the other kids.

Part of the reason had been that she had no parents in a town where two-parent families were still the norm, and those kinds of differences always set children apart. Another reason had been that Poppy had a reputation as a mean grouch and all the kids in town were slightly scared of him.

However, those kids were adults now and eager to be friends with the big-city television star. And Francine found it impossible to hold a grudge. They had all just been kids.

As the cowbell over the diner door clanged, she looked up to see Travis enter. Immediately her back stiffened. She hadn't seen him except in passing since the evening they shared the kiss in the cornfield.

She had spent the couple of days since that incident studiously not thinking about it. But as she greeted him, her lips tingled, as if remembering the warmth and pleasure of that kiss.

"You look like you're hard at work," he said with a warm smile.

"You mean I look like I'm hardly working," she returned as she stood and went around the counter.

He slid onto a stool opposite where she stood. "Can I get a cup of coffee?"

"Sure, although you can't order anything from the kitchen. It's officially closed." She turned to grab a cup and the coffeepot.

"How about a piece of apple pie?"

"No problem," she replied as she poured his coffee, then served him his dessert request.

"Francine, I'm leaving!" Benny yelled from the back room.

"Okay, Benny. Good night," she returned.

"Why don't you sit down and finish your coffee with me while I eat my pie?" Travis suggested.

Francine hesitated, then nodded. "All right." She grabbed her mug and walked around the counter to sit on the stool next to him.

"Nobody makes apple pie like Benny," Travis said after taking a bite of the fruity pastry. His eyes crinkled at the corners as a smile curved his lips. "Remember that pie you made when you were a junior in high school?"

A burst of laughter exploded from Francine. "Oh, how can I forget? We were both sick for a week."

"I've never had such a bad stomachache."

"I thought the apples were supposed to be green." She smiled at him. "I don't suppose it helped that I'd only baked it a half an hour and we each ate half the pie.''

His smile deepened, enriched by their shared memories. ''We had some good times, didn't we, Francine?''

''The best.''

There was a long silence, but it wasn't an uncomfortable one. Rather, it was the companionable silence of two people remembering pleasant times.

Travis took another bite, sipped his coffee, then looked at her once again. ''Tell me about New York, Frannie.''

She looked at him in surprise. ''What do you want to know?''

''I want to know about where you live, your work...if it's all lived up to your expectations.'' His gaze held hers intently.

''We have a nice apartment on the Upper West Side. Nothing fancy, but it's home.'' She looked down into her mug, unable to hold his gaze. She couldn't tell him she'd lost the apartment, that she'd been unable to pay the rent on the tiny studio even by working two part-time jobs.

''The city itself is unbelievable,'' she continued. ''There's an undercurrent of excitement all the time, a frenzied pace that's contagious.'' She didn't mention the fear, the coldness of the metropolis, the loneliness she felt so often, despite the crowds of people. ''It's an exciting place to live,'' she finished.

What she wanted to tell him was that it hadn't lived up to her dreams...at least not yet. Living in New York, trying to find work, all of it was far more difficult than she'd ever dreamed. But there was an element of pride that refused to confess these things to him.

"What about you? Tell me about your life. What have you been doing over the last five years?" she said, wanting to turn the topic away from herself.

He shrugged. "There's not much to tell. I lead a pretty simple life. I work the fields, visit Poppy, occasionally do a little fishing, and sometimes see a movie. I'm sure it sounds quite boring compared to your life."

"Not really," she protested. She got up and went around the counter and grabbed the coffee pot to refill their cups.

"I'm sure Poppy appreciates you helping out here," he said.

Francine sat back down. "To be honest, I'm enjoying it. For the most part, I never minded working here." She grinned. "Glenda Snider came in the other day. It broke my heart to see the head cheerleader sporting an extra fifty pounds and looking so frazzled as she tangled with her three kids."

Travis laughed. "Broke your heart? I'll just bet. You're wicked, Francine."

"Wicked?" She shook her head. "No, just human. Glenda was one of the meanest girls in high school. I can't help feeling a little vindicated that she's not a glamour girl anymore."

"I figured you would have gotten your vindication years ago when you served her pie à la Glenda."

Francine laughed, knowing exactly what he was talking about. One afternoon after school, Glenda and her minions had come into the diner. As usual, as Francine served them, they'd been rude and hateful.

Francine, fed up with the bunch of them, had managed to "accidentally" tilt Glenda's pie à la mode as she served her, causing the large scoop of ice cream to fall into Glenda's lap.

Her laughter faded, and she gazed at Travis, remembering more of that particular story. "She was so angry she went home and told her big brother, who threatened to beat me up."

Travis nodded. "And I told him if he touched a hair on your head, I'd mop up Main Street with him." His eyes held hers, speaking the language of old camaraderie.

"We were quite a pair," Francine said with a rueful shake of her head. She tilted her head, her gaze steady on him. "I can't imagine what my life might have been like without you in it," she said truthfully, knowing how utterly bleak her childhood would have been without his being a part of it.

"I guess it was just a matter of survival for us. The old you-and-me-against-the-world mentality. And then we grew up."

"Yes. We grew up." She slid off the stool and went back around the counter. Too many emotions swept through her, too many memories assailed her. This was dangerous, this walk down memory lane.

"Did you know Poppy had a heart attack soon after you left?"

Francine nearly dropped the coffeepot at his words. "What?"

Travis finished the last of his pie and shoved the plate aside. "He was in the hospital for a week. That's when I started taking over the work in his fields."

Francine felt as if her world, her very reality, had suddenly tilted. Poppy ill? She couldn't remember him ever being sick. Her heart convulsed at the mental image she got of him in a hospital bed, all alone, without any family to help him. "But he's all right now?" she asked anxiously.

"He seems to be fine," Travis agreed. "Don't worry, I'm sure he won't try to make you stay by using guilt."

Francine stiffened her back. "Are you trying to make me feel guilty about leaving?" She filled the sink with soapy water, then plunged the glass coffee carafe into the suds. "Is that why you told me about his heart attack? Or are you trying to manipulate me into staying here now?"

"I'm not trying to do either," Travis said, a note of irritation rising in his voice. "I just thought you should know Poppy hasn't been well."

"I'm sorry Poppy has been ill, but his health isn't going to stop me from leaving here and returning to my life in New York." She swished a dishcloth around inside the coffee carafe. "He's survived without me for five years, he'll survive when I'm gone again." Besides, Poppy seemed well enough now, she told herself.

"Right. Heaven help anyone who gets in the way of Francine Webster and her dreams of stardom."

Suddenly any remnants of camaraderie, any lingering memories of old friendship, of lost love, were gone, banished beneath the weight of his words and the bitterness in his voice.

She turned from the sink and looked at him. "You know what I think, Travis? I think you're jealous because I had the courage to walk away from here five years ago and try to make a better life for myself." All the hurt she'd kept inside bubbled up, transforming to anger.

He stood, his shoulders stiff and a muscle throbbing at the corner of his jaw. "And you're angry because I didn't go with you. Because for the first time in our lives, I told you no. I had a mother depending on me, and two little sisters who needed me here."

"Excuses," she returned angrily. "Face the truth, Travis. You were a coward." She heard his swift intake of breath at her words, saw the flash of danger in his eyes, but she didn't care. She'd had five years to ruminate on the fact that Travis hadn't loved her enough to leave with her. "You were afraid to leave here, afraid to spread your wings and fly. I flew...and I intend to continue to fly."

"That's the old Francine I remember," he replied as he pulled his wallet out of his pocket and tossed a couple of dollars on the counter. "Never pulling punches, always lashing out at those who care about her."

"Oh, please, tell me again how much Poppy cared about me when I was young. Tell me about all the love he showed me with his silences, with his strict rules. Raising me was his duty, a duty he just tolerated, nothing more." She grabbed his plate and cup and added them to her soapy water, then turned back to him. "And let's talk about how much you cared for me. Face it, Travis. What we felt for each other had nothing to do with love. I needed somebody to care about me, and you fed on my anger because you were too much of a coward to feel angry yourself."

"That's twice you've called me a coward, Francine," he said, his eyes narrowed and his voice ominously soft. "I know who I am, and I know what I am, and the choices I made had nothing to do with cowardice."

He started for the door, his hands clenching and unclenching at his sides. When he reached the door, he turned back to her, his eyes still dark with suppressed anger. "I told you before not to stay here too long, Francine. I think you've already overstayed your visit." With those words, the cowbell rang discordantly as he slammed out the door.

Francine fought her impulse to throw the wet dish towel at his back and instead stomped over to the door, flipped the Open sign to Closed, then locked herself in.

As she walked back toward the counter, her vision blurred with tears, she blinked them back and bit the inside of her cheek. She'd never been a crier, but she'd never felt more like crying than at this very moment.

She'd said things she didn't intend to say, hurtful, hateful things that left a bitter taste in her mouth. But he'd responded in kind, making her sound selfish and thoughtless while loathing shone from his eyes.

How had a simple conversation over a piece of apple pie gotten so out of control? What had begun as a pleasant walk back into the past had been transformed to an ugly screaming match of old wounds.

She finished washing the last of the dishes, then dried her hands and once again sat at the counter, too upset to go directly home.

The information about Poppy's heart attack sent a

chill through her. Poppy had always seemed so strong, so indestructible. She'd always believed he was too darn mean for heaven to want him, and too cranky for hell to want to keep him.

But he's fine now, she told herself again. It wasn't like she was leaving him sick and helpless. He appeared as strong, as capable, as he'd ever been. There was no reason for her to change her plans.

She knew much of the reason the conversation with Travis had gotten out of control, that the whole thing had escalated was because somehow, some way, despite her intentions to the contrary, she cared about what Travis thought of her. And from the conversation they'd just had, she realized it wasn't much.

Travis couldn't remember the last time he'd been so angry, then realized he had never in his life been this angry before.

As he drove home, he drew deep breaths, trying to get his emotions under control. How was it she still managed to crawl under his skin so effectively? Why did he care at all what she thought of him?

A coward. The word rang in his ears, and he tightened his grip on the steering wheel as a renewed burst of anger surged through him. She thought he'd been a coward because he hadn't run away with her to fulfill her dreams. Her dreams, not his.

He suspected now that all the times they were together, talking of what they wanted, she'd never really heard his dreams.

On impulse, instead of driving directly home, he turned in the direction of his sister's house. Her husband worked the late shift and didn't get home until midnight, so he knew Susie would be up waiting for her husband's arrival home.

As he expected, when he pulled into the driveway of the neat, cozy ranch house on the corner, lights burned in the living room window.

He shut off his engine, but remained seated in the truck, trying to cast off the last of his anger before going inside. Damn Francine. For the first time in years, he found himself questioning the decisions he'd made so long ago, wondering if perhaps a touch of cowardice had played a role in those decisions.

Had he been afraid to leave the small town? Had he been scared to take off into the unknown?

With a muttered curse, he got out of the truck and walked to the front door. Before he could knock, Susie opened the door with an expression of surprised pleasure on her face. "Travis, I thought that was your truck." She reached up and kissed him on his cheek. "Come in. Is everything all right?"

"Everything is fine," he assured her. "I just finished having coffee and pie at the diner and decided on impulse to stop by."

"I'm so glad you did. You know I always love to see my favorite brother." She smiled and gestured him into the living room.

"Need I remind you that it's easy to be a favorite brother when I'm the only one?" Travis said dryly.

Susie laughed as they sat down side by side on the overstuffed sofa. "Now, tell me the real reason you're here." Her gaze looked him over analytically.

"What do you mean?"

She smiled prettily. "Travis, I love you, but you

can't fool me. Something is bothering you. I can see it in your eyes."

Travis leaned back against the cushions and raked a hand through his hair. "Did you know that five years ago, when Francine left town, she wanted me to go with her?"

Again Susie smiled. "Travis, there wasn't much that went on between you and Francine that Margaret and I weren't aware of." She frowned thoughtfully. "We were terrified that you'd go with her."

He looked at her in surprise. "Neither of you ever said a word to me."

She shrugged. "It wasn't our place to try to make your decision for you. But we prayed every night that Francine wouldn't talk you into going."

Travis was completely shocked at her words. He'd never dreamed his two younger sisters had any indication what was going on in his life, the decisions he was faced with at that time. "Why didn't you tell me you were afraid? Tell me not to go?"

Susie leaned her head back against the sofa, her dark eyes not wavering from his. "Margaret wanted to. She was only thirteen and was scared of what would happen to us if you left. But I told her you had to make your own decision. I didn't want you to stay because you were forced to. I wanted it to be a choice you made of free will. I didn't want it to be duty that kept you with us. I wanted it to be love."

"I can't figure out how you got so smart," Travis exclaimed, his heart swelling with love for her.

She smiled. "I just never wanted you to be sorry for the choice you made." She hesitated a moment. "Are you sorry?"

Travis pulled her toward him and gave her a hug. "No. I've regretted lots of things, but staying here and remaining a part of your life and Margaret's has never been one of them."

"You were our anchor, Travis," Susie said as he released her. "Dad was gone, we knew Mom was dying. You made us feel safe."

This was why he'd stopped here, he thought as warmth suffused him. Her words were merely reconfirming what he'd known. He hadn't stayed because he was a coward.

He'd remained behind because his family needed him and he loved his sisters, knew he was all they had. Yes, he'd felt duty-bound, but it had been duty bred in love.

"It had to be tough on you," Susie continued. "Being only fifteen when Dad died, then by the time you were twenty-two finding yourself mother and father to two young girls. You gave up so much to be there for all of us."

"I didn't give up anything," he protested gruffly.

"You gave up football games and dances, nights out with your friends, and all those things young men do," Susie protested. "I know how the other kids teased you, Travis. I remember how they called you a mama's boy because you always had to hurry home to take care of her, then later had to hurry home to take care of us."

"It wasn't a big deal," he replied. And with the distance of the years, it wasn't, although at the time it was happening, it had been hurtful. Francine was right about one thing—he'd fed vicariously off the anger she so easily exhibited.

"I'd better get out of here," Travis said, his heart much lighter than it had been when he arrived. "It's getting late, and your hubby will be home anytime." He stood, and Susie got up to follow him to the front door.

"Travis, I've got one little bit of news to tell you before you go."

"What's that?" Travis asked.

"You're going to be an uncle."

Travis stared at her in surprise. Then, with a whoop of joy, he wrapped her in a bear hug. "When?"

Susie laughed. "Not for a while, I'm only eight weeks pregnant. If it's a girl, we're going to name her Mary Elizabeth...after Mama. If it's a boy, we want to call him Richard Travis after you."

Travis felt that if his heart got any bigger in his chest, it would block off all of his breathing. He touched his sister's cheek softly, then turned and went out the door, too filled with emotion to say anything.

Minutes later, as he drove home, his heart still sang with the news of Susie's pregnancy and the fact that they wanted to name a boy after him.

If ever he'd entertained any doubts whatsoever about his decision to remain behind years ago, this news banished every one. This was what life was about...family, love...births.

Birth. It seemed odd that his baby sister would become a parent before he did. He was twenty-four years old, and at the rate he was going, he'd never have his own child, would share only in the joy of his sisters' children. And having a family had been his dream, the one he shared with Francine, the one he suspected she either hadn't heard or hadn't wanted to hear.

By the time he pulled into his own driveway, his anger with Francine had waned. It wasn't her fault that their dreams had taken them in separate directions. And it wasn't his fault, either. It was a shame they had spent their time together this evening beating each other up over issues long past and impossible to change.

He now faced the fact that a large chunk of his heart would forever belong to Francine. She'd taken it from him a little piece at a time, beginning on that first night, when he was eleven and she was ten and he saw her sneaking out of her bedroom window.

He got out of his truck and stood on his porch, his gaze sweeping across to the house nearby. Francine's car was parked out front, letting him know she'd gotten home from the diner safe and sound. His gaze moved up to the second-floor window he knew was her bedroom.

Yes, she would always hold a piece of his heart, but it was time for him to finally move on, to get past Francine Webster and those sweet memories and dreams of what might have been.

It was time he took an active role in making his own dreams come true. All he had to do was figure out exactly where to begin.

Chapter Six

Sooner or later, she was going to have to apologize to him. Francine's harsh words to Travis haunted her all day following their argument, and she knew she wouldn't rest until she told him she was sorry. She'd never been able to stand the thought that Travis might be angry with her.

He didn't come by after dinner, as had become his custom, and Francine was surprised to realize she missed him. She missed listening to the deep tones of Poppy and Travis talking on the porch while she cleaned up the kitchen. She missed Gretchen's giggles, which Travis always seemed to provoke so easily.

When Poppy had gone to bed and Gretchen was asleep, Francine sat at her bedroom window, staring out at Travis's house. She could see a light on in his living room, so she knew he hadn't gone to bed yet.

She hadn't meant to call him a coward, knowing

in her heart that cowardice wasn't what had kept him from going with her to New York. But it was easier to believe it was the fear of the unknown that had kept him here than to acknowledge what she knew to be the real reason...that he simply hadn't loved her enough.

Even now, after all this time, that thought caused an ache to pierce through her heart. She'd often wondered what quality about herself was so singularly unlovable. Why was it that the two people who mattered most in her life hadn't been able to love her enough? First Poppy, then Travis...neither had been able to show her the all-consuming, unconditional love she'd desperately needed.

For so long, she'd been angry about it, but she was surprised now to feel no anger, just a deep sadness. After all, she couldn't be mad at them; they couldn't command emotions they didn't feel.

Still, she didn't want Travis to feel the weight of her bitter words. She should go over to his house, clear the air between them and request a truce for the remainder of her time in Cooperville.

As she considered this course of action, the light in his living room went out. Too late to make amends tonight, Francine told herself.

She watched the darkened house for several long minutes, knowing she should go to bed and get some sleep, but her heart was too heavy for rest. She didn't want Travis to avoid coming over because of their argument. It wasn't fair for him to punish Poppy and Gretchen because she'd lost her temper.

She sighed, her gaze going from Travis's house to the full moon overhead. It looked like a big, fat smiling face. Or a distant spotlight. Suddenly she remembered her dream from the night before.

She'd been onstage performing, and when the curtain fell, the crowd had begun to chant. "Frannie." "Frannie." "Frannie." She'd run back on stage, holding out her hands toward the audience as if to embrace them. She'd felt their love reaching out to her, warming her, filling up the empty spaces in her heart.

When she finally awakened, a smile had still curved her lips and a renewed determination had flowed through her, a determination to get back to New York and achieve her goals.

She again looked at Travis's house, realizing a light now shone from his bedroom window. He was obviously going to bed. She tried to stifle her need to apologize to him, realizing she should be asleep. She was working the morning shift, and it was already nearing midnight. She started to turn away from her window, but hesitated as another thought nudged her brain.

It had worked so many years before. Would it still work? She grabbed the flashlight from the nightstand drawer and went back to the window.

Memories flooded through her, memories of hundreds of nights from her past, when she'd signaled Travis with the flashlight and they'd met in the nearby cornfield.

As she watched, his bedroom light blinked off, plunging his house into total darkness. If he went directly to bed, he wouldn't see her signal. If, for some reason, he glanced out his window, he would see it. But would he come?

She aimed the flashlight toward his house, then turned it on and off, on and off. Two short bursts of light, their code to meet. She waited a moment... another moment...then signaled again.

He's probably in bed, she thought, her heart heavy with disappointment. Why would he be looking out his window at this time of night?

Her heart expanded when she saw a flash of beaming light returning her beacon. Two short beams in answer to hers. She set the flashlight down, her heart suddenly pounding in the ancient rhythm of anticipation.

She didn't even consider going downstairs and out the front door. Old habits deeply ingrained dictated her actions as she slid the window up and quietly removed the screen. Sneaking out the window had always been the way she met Travis, and all the excitement she'd once felt at the expectation of seeing him returned as she climbed out and grabbed the solid wooden trellis.

Thank goodness Poppy had stopped planting roses years ago and had never taken down the sturdy trellis. Otherwise, the climb down would have been hampered by the thorny flowers.

Years of experience came back to her as she nimbly made her way to the ground. And for the first time in months...years...her heart felt young again, free, as she hit the ground and ran toward the waving cornstalks.

They'd always met in the same row, the same general place, and when she reached it, she stopped, tried to catch her breath as she waited for him.

Like an illuminated plump honeydew melon, the

full moon spilled down shimmering light. Francine drew a deep breath, wondering why her heart continued to race.

This meeting wasn't like the ones in the past, when she and Travis couldn't wait to be in each other's arms. At that time, the cornfield had been the only place they could escape his little sisters. And the late hours were the only time Travis wasn't working in the fields, or chopping wood, or doing chores to maintain the farm for his family.

She sank to the ground, where the musty scent of rich earth and growing corn surrounded her. She was here to tell him she was sorry for the hateful words she'd said. She was here to make peace with him. That was all.

She heard him before she saw him, heard the swish and rustle of the corn as he moved through it. She stood, the beat of her heart accelerating, although she didn't understand why.

He appeared in front of her, wearing only a pair of low-slung jeans and shoes. His hair gleamed with dampness, and she could smell a minty soap scent that let her know he'd apparently just gotten out of the shower.

She smiled a tentative greeting. "I wasn't sure you'd come."

"I'm here." He thrust his hands in his pockets and shrugged. "I'd just showered and was getting ready to climb into bed when I saw the flash of light." He tilted his head and eyed her curiously. "Everything all right?"

"Fine." Francine bit her bottom lip and frowned. "Actually, it isn't fine. Travis, I said some awful

things to you last night at the diner and I needed to
tell you I'm sorry.''

"We both were a little out of line," he said easily.

"Yes, but you know me, I tend to go for the jugular
when I get angry.''

He smiled, his dark eyes gleaming silvery in the
moonlight. "I wouldn't recognize you any other
way.''

She returned his smile, the tightness in her chest
easing as she realized she'd been forgiven. "We
missed you tonight after supper," she said.

"I went into town to visit with Susie and her husband.'' He pulled his hands out of his pockets and
raked one through his hair. "She's pregnant, and so
we had a little celebration.''

"Oh, that's wonderful," Francine exclaimed.
"You must be thrilled.''

"I am." Again he flashed his smile, and warmth
spread through Francine's body. Travis's smile had
always done that to her. "If it's a boy, they're going
to name him after me.''

"Oh, Travis, I'm so happy for you." Francine
forced herself to ignore her impulse to throw her arms
around his neck in congratulations. Someplace, in the
very back of her head, she knew that if she touched
him in any way, she would be on dangerous ground.
"The other day Poppy mentioned that you should
have a houseful of children of your own.''

His smile faded, and his eyes glittered intently as
he held her gaze. "I always thought that's the way it
would be. That you'd have my children.''

For a moment, his words hung between them. His
bare chest gleamed in the moonlight, looking warm

and firm. She could remember the feel of those muscles beneath her fingertips. "I always told you what my dream was," she finally said softly. She broke her gaze from his and stared up at the moon. "You always knew what was important to me."

"Yeah, but I always thought it was just youthful talk. You know, like little girls who dreamed of being ballerinas or little boys wanting to be firemen. You wanted to be a star."

Francine wrapped her arms around herself, wanting to change the subject, knowing they flirted with disaster when the discussion turned to dreams and the past. "So when is Susie due?"

"Sometime the last of March." Again he shoved his hands in his pockets, his jeans lowering to show a provocative expanse of skin. "It will be nice to have a baby in the family. Susie says she wants a big family, four or five kids."

"And what about Margaret? Does she want lots of children, too?"

He nodded. "Eventually. Right now she's focused on getting her teaching degree. But she's always said she wants a big family."

"Do you still have your guitar?" she asked.

"Yeah, although it's been a while since I've played."

"I used to love to hear you play and sing." She remembered the sound of his voice, smooth and deep. Even Poppy had occasionally joined them on the porch on the nights when Travis would bring his guitar over and sing old ballads. "You were as good as any of the successful singers performing today."

He smiled again. "The difference, Francine, is that

I never wanted to be a performing artist. All I ever wanted was to someday be able to sing lullabies to my children.''

An ache filled Francine as she thought of Travis holding Gretchen in his arms and singing sweet lullabies to her.

Had she remained in Cooperville, would that have been the case? Would she and Travis have built a life together? She wasn't sure. They'd both been so young, and Travis had been overwhelmed by the responsibilities of his sick mother and his young sisters. There hadn't been room in his life for a young bride and a baby.

No, she'd done the right thing in leaving and not telling him about Gretchen. He'd had too many responsibilities at that time. And now it was far too late.

''I'd better get back,'' she said. ''I just felt like it was important that we declare a truce for the rest of the time I'm here.''

He nodded. ''There's a carnival coming to town this weekend. Why don't we all go together and spend Saturday having fun? Gretchen would have a ball.''

Francine hesitated. ''Okay,'' she finally said, despite her misgivings about spending an entire day with Travis. ''Betty said something about it. She was moaning about the fact that it will be slow at the diner, since everyone will be at the carnival, so she gave me the day off. What time should we plan on?''

''I'll pick you up about eleven.''

''We'll be ready.'' She started to leave, but stopped as he placed a hand on her arm. She turned back to look at him, and instantly she knew the dangerous ground had jumped up to slap her in the face.

His eyes sparked with an emotion she recognized because she felt it herself. Desire. Pure and simple, it flooded through her as he wrapped her in his arms. As his mouth claimed hers, she realized it was the anticipation of this happening that had set her heart to racing the moment she climbed out her window.

Hot and eager, his lips plied hers, and she didn't even think of objecting. Instead, she opened her mouth to him, allowing him to deepen the kiss as her hands caressed the warm, hard muscles of his chest.

His skin was just as she'd remembered, warm to the touch, the flesh soft, but covering the firm strength of muscle. She reveled in the feel of it, splaying her fingertips against him.

Somewhere in the back of her mind, she knew they shouldn't be doing this, but she didn't want to stop. She knew that when she was back in New York, lonely and miserable, it would be the memory of Travis's kiss that sustained her.

As the kiss lingered, he pulled her more firmly against him, one hand moving up beneath her blouse to cover her bra-clad breast. She could feel the heat of his hand, felt the tightening of her nipple as it stiffened in response.

Liquid fire flowed through her veins, creating a burning flame inside her that only he could quell. Her hands roamed freely across his back, remembering the feel of the warm skin as they repeated the experience of the tactile contact from years ago.

When he finally broke the kiss, her breath came rapidly, raggedly, from her throat. He moaned as his lips trailed down the length of her throat, pausing to taste the flesh in the hollow of her neck. With surprising agility, his fingers worked the buttons of her blouse until they were all undone, and then he moved his hand to her back and unsnapped her bra.

Pure, undiluted pleasure soared through her as he gently pushed her bra up and covered her breast with his bare hand. He dipped his head down and touched her turgid nipple with his tongue. She gasped at this new intimacy, and her knees nearly buckled as passion grew hotter.

He straightened, his mouth once again claiming hers as his hips thrust into hers, allowing her to recognize his complete arousal. "Frannie..." he whispered in her ear, his breath warm and causing a shiver of want to race up her spine. "Come home with me. Come home with me and let me love you."

His words caused memories to burst in her head, memories of that single night when she'd given herself completely to him. She remembered how he'd filled her up, body and soul, how their heartbeats had matched each other in rhythm as they experienced making love for the very first time.

She wanted that again, ached with wanting it again. But she knew she'd be a fool to allow this to go any further. For the first time since he'd touched her, survival battled with desire. "Travis..." She pushed him away and stepped back from him, her legs threatening to fold beneath her. "This is madness," she said, unsurprised to hear her voice reedy and thin. She couldn't look at him, and instead focused on refastening her bra and buttoning her blouse.

She finally looked up at him. "I'm sorry, I shouldn't have let things go as far as they did."

He released a deep sigh. "You weren't exactly

alone," he replied. "And you're right. We were about to make a major mistake."

Despite the fact that halting the lovemaking had been the right choice, an arrow of disappointment shot through her at his words. Even though she knew it would have been a big mistake, irrationally she didn't want him to feel that way. "I'm going back to New York in a couple of weeks. Nothing could come from us making love," she said.

"You're right," he agreed, then flashed her a tight smile. "Except that it would relieve my want." He drew a deep breath. "I won't lie to you, Francine. I want you. We were good together before, and I just thought it might be nice to repeat the experience."

His words caused an ache to build in her heart. What she felt when he held her, when he kissed her, had had little to do with "nice." For her, it hadn't been simply the need to duplicate a good time. It had been something deeper, more profound.

But once again his words caused her to remember why she'd left. He'd never loved her enough. And nothing had changed with the passing of the years.

"I've got to get back. I don't want Gretchen to wake up and wonder where I've gone," she said.

"I'll see you Saturday morning," he replied.

She nodded and turned to leave. This time he didn't stop her, and as she walked toward the house, her body ached with unfulfillment and her heart hurt with the knowledge that it hadn't been love that prompted his kisses, his caresses. It had been lust, the memory of a good sexual experience.

Lust had certainly been a part of what she felt, but it hadn't been all she felt. She knew that if she'd made love to Travis again, she might not want to leave Cooperville.

But there was nothing for her here. Poppy had always just barely tolerated her. Her peers had always made fun of her. And though she believed Travis had once cared for her deeply, might still care about her welfare, it was obvious he hadn't loved her enough to ask her to stay. Not in the past. And not now.

She had to leave, go back to New York and try to achieve her dreams. Because deep in her heart, she knew that without her dreams, she had nothing.

Travis watched her go, creeping closer to her house to watch as she climbed the rose trellis, back up to her bedroom. Long after she disappeared into the room and the light went off, he remained at the edge of the cornfield.

He wanted to hate her, had tried hating her for the past five years. But hate wasn't an emotion that came easily to him, especially where Frannie was concerned.

If he believed that making love to her would make her stay, he would have seduced her every moment of every day. He could have seduced her moments earlier, knew that if he pushed just a little bit he could have made her forget her weak protest.

She'd wanted him. He'd felt it in her quickened breath, in the way she arched against him, in the heat of her body pressed against his. He'd felt her desire in the honeyed sweetness of her kisses, in her fingers as she'd touched his chest.

Yes, he might have seduced her, if he'd thought it would change her plans. But that was the mistaken

SILHOUETTE®

WITH OUR
COMPLIMENTS

THE EDITORS

THE EDITOR'S "THANK YOU" FREE GIFTS INCLUDE:

▶ Four BRAND-NEW romance novels
▶ PLUS — a Cuddly Teddy Bear

PLACE FREE GIFT SEAL HERE

YES! I have placed my Editor's "thank you" seal in the space provided above. Please send me 4 free books and a Cuddly Teddy Bear. I understand I am under no obligation to purchase any books, as explained on the back and on the opposite page.

215 CIS CCQL (U-SIL-R-11/97)

NAME

ADDRESS   APT.

CITY   STATE   ZIP

Thank you!

DETACH AND MAIL CARD TODAY!

THE SILHOUETTE READER SERVICE™: HERE'S HOW IT WORKS

Accepting free books places you under no obligation to buy anything. You may keep the books and gift and return the shipping statement marked "cancel". If you do not cancel, about a month later we will send you 6 additional novels, and bill you just $2.67 each plus 25¢ delivery per book and applicable sales tax, if any*. That's the complete price, and—compared to cover prices of $3.25 each—quite a bargain! You may cancel at any time, but if you choose to continue, every month we'll send you 6 more books, which you may either purchase at the discount price…or return to us and cancel your subscription.

*Terms and prices subject to change without notice. Sales tax applicable in N.Y.

belief he'd had years before. He'd been certain that if they made love, she'd never be able to leave him. And he'd been wrong.

He knew he'd hurt her with his words about wanting to repeat their pleasant experience again. The words had sounded cold, unemotional, as he uttered them, but he'd had to salvage a little of his pride.

God help him, he wanted to hate her. It would be such a clean, uncomplicated emotion, compared to what he felt for her at this moment. It would be so much easier to deal with hate than to know that he loved her...and would never have her.

Chapter Seven

Saturday morning dawned bright and beautiful, a perfect day for a carnival. Francine awoke earlier than usual, surprised to be up before Poppy. She made a pot of coffee, then carried a cup to the front porch.

The last of the sunrise lingered in the east, while the rest of the sky had the brilliance of a newly sharpened crayon the color of a bird's egg.

Francine sipped her coffee slowly, allowing the porch swing to move gently to and fro. She should feel content, happy. She almost had enough money saved for her and Gretchen to head back to New York.

She figured another week, two at the most, and they could be on their way. She should be ecstatic, but she wasn't.

These past couple of weeks had been relatively happy ones, more so than she'd ever dreamed possible. She and Poppy, while not especially warm to each other, seemed to have come to reluctant terms with each other. She'd learned to expect very little from him, and as a result she wasn't disappointed.

Gretchen helped, filling in any silences that might linger between the old man and Francine, creating laughter where none had existed before.

The first time Francine heard Poppy's laughter, she'd nearly fallen out of her chair. Although rusty and gruff, it had not been an unpleasant sound and it had filled Francine with a wistful pleasure. She'd felt as if she'd been handed an unexpected gift.

Again she found herself wondering why Gretchen seemed to be able to so easily reach in and touch Poppy's heart, while Francine had spent her entire youth trying to get one little smile, a single kind word, from the man who raised her.

It was one of those things that would forever remain a mystery to her. Just like the mystery of how Travis could desire her, want to make love to her, but not be in love with her.

She shoved these thoughts aside, determined to enjoy the day with no haunting regrets from the past, no disturbing questions about the future, to torment her.

She was tired of whining about her past. Her childhood had been worse than some, better than some. She'd been clothed and fed, kept warm and safe. Some children didn't even have that much.

As far as Travis was concerned, she'd had one night of exquisite love, the soul-searing, heart-bonding kind that some women never, ever experienced in their lives. She was tired of being angry and hurt about her past and had decided instead to count her blessings.

It was a beautiful day, and she intended to spend it with a handsome man and her precious daughter. What more could she want?

She turned as the door creaked open and Poppy stepped out on the porch, a cup of coffee in hand. "You're up early," he said as he eased himself down in the lounge chair across from the swing.

"It's too pretty a morning to laze about in bed," she answered.

"Hmm, looks like a hundred other mornings to me," he replied, with his usual touch of cantankerousness.

Francine ignored him, refusing to allow his grouchiness to spoil her pleasure in the gorgeous morning. For a few minutes silence reigned between them, as both of them drank their coffee.

For a change, it wasn't a silence Francine resented. She'd come to realize in the past couple of days that Poppy was generally a man of few words. He spoke when he had something to say, but rarely filled silences with meaningless social chatter.

"Poppy, the other night Travis told me that you had a heart attack right after I left here," she said, breaking the silence as she remembered Travis's words.

He frowned. "That man should mind his own business and not be talking about mine."

She eyed his face searchingly. "Why didn't you write me? You had my address. Why didn't you let me know you were sick?"

He looked at her, his eyes a faded blue, but still as

sharp as ever. "What could you have done? Last I heard, you hadn't graduated medical school."

Francine bit her tongue for a moment. "Besides," he continued, "it wasn't a bad one. I was up and around in no time."

Francine wanted to tell him he should have written her because she cared what happened to him. He should have let her know because, despite the fact that he'd made it clear he'd never considered her anything but a burden, she'd loved him. Still loved him. This realization surprised her.

For a moment, she couldn't speak, as she embraced the fact that she loved the crotchety old man. He was the only parent she'd ever have, the father of the mother she'd lost. He and Gretchen comprised the sum of her family, and she realized that despite their past, there was a bond between them that neither of them could ever dispel.

"Travis and I are taking Gretchen into town this morning. There's a carnival set up in the field behind the grocery store. You want to come with us?" It was the best she could do, as much as she could afford. She couldn't blurt out that she loved him, refused to give him the power to hurt her. But she could offer an olive branch in the form of an invitation to join them for the day.

"A carnival? A bunch of damned-fool nonsense," he said with a scowl. Francine frowned. She should have known better than to offer. "I suppose I'd better go with you, so those carny sharpies don't take you for every cent you have," he continued. "Besides, Miss Beans will probably want me to ride one of them rides with her."

Joy filled Francine's heart, although again she wondered why he was able to give to Gretchen what he'd never been able to give to her. Still, she shoved that thought aside, realizing it was going to be a day of memories. A day with Travis, Poppy and Gretchen together. A family day that would linger in her heart long after she'd left Cooperville and Travis and Poppy behind.

Several hours later, they were all in Travis's car as he drove them toward town. Gretchen chattered like a magpie, excited at the new adventure that awaited her. She'd never been to a carnival before, and she thought the whole thing sounded exciting.

Poppy sat next to her in the back seat, grunting answers to all her questions. "I know what a carousel is," she exclaimed proudly. "We rode on one last year in Central Park, didn't we, Mommy?"

"Yes, honey, we did," Francine replied.

"Poppy, you'll ride the carousel with me, won't you?" Gretchen asked. "We'll find you a real pretty horse to ride, with a big blue ribbon to match your eyes."

Poppy snorted. "Then we'll have to look for a horse full of beans for you to ride," he said, making Gretchen laugh.

As Poppy and Gretchen talked in the back seat, Francine leaned her head against the seat and wondered if a day could be more perfect.

Travis had greeted them with a pleasant smile that told Francine he'd put their suspended intimacy in the cornfield out of his mind and intended to simply enjoy the day. And it was a beautiful day. A slight breeze took the edge off the late-August heat, making it pleasant to be outside.

She cast a surreptitious glance at Travis. He looked relaxed and happy, as if he expected this day to be pleasant. She wrapped her arms around her shoulders, wishing she could embrace this moment and hold it in her heart forever.

As Travis turned his car onto Main Street, the sights and sounds of the carnival beckoned. Behind the grocery store rose the upper portion of the Ferris wheel, and the air was redolent with the scents of fresh popcorn, simmering hot dogs and cotton candy.

"Oh, this is going to be such fun," Gretchen exclaimed as they walked from their parking spot toward the carnival entrance.

"You'd better hang on to my hand so you don't get lost," Poppy told her sternly. Gretchen slipped her small hand into his, and the sight caused Francine's heart to expand.

"Mommy, you have to hold Travis's hand so you don't get lost," Gretchen said.

"Oh, no…" Francine started to protest.

"I think that's a splendid idea," Travis interjected, and took Francine's hand. "The buddy system is always smart in a crowd."

His hand was warm as it enclosed hers. Although it was bigger, stronger, Francine still felt as if their hands had been made to fit together.

With Gretchen and Poppy in the lead, they walked down the midway, looking on either side at the sights offered by tent after tent of games of chance and skill, and ride after ride for children and adults.

Francine shot a sideways glance at Travis, admiring

his sheer handsomeness. Clad in jeans and in a pale blue short-sleeved sports shirt that provided the perfect foil for his dark hair and eyes, he looked every inch the confident, successful farmer out for a day of enjoyment.

As they walked, they ran into people they knew, stopping to chat with one, then another. For the first time, Francine realized the sense of community, of benevolent warmth, that seemed inherent in a small town.

The kids who were cruel to her in high school had grown up, matured, and they greeted her with genuine friendliness, as if those earlier years had never happened.

Francine found herself both delighted and confused by their warmth. Was it because they all thought she was a big movie star come home for a brief vacation? Or was it simply that youth had fled, and with it the silly childish intolerance and prejudices that had once seemed important?

When Poppy and Gretchen got on the carousel, she mentioned her thoughts to Travis. "Have I changed, or have they?" she asked.

He smiled and waved at Gretchen and Poppy as the carousel carried them around. "I think it's a combination of both," he answered. His gaze was warm as he focused on her. "I think we brought on some of it, Francine. You and I were so tight, we had little room for anyone else. I've often wondered if maybe we didn't unintentionally push people away, then get angry when they didn't get close."

"Maybe you're right," she agreed thoughtfully. "Part of me wanted other friends, but a stronger part of me wanted only you. I was afraid other people would mess up what we had.''

He nodded, his smile remaining but turning wistful. ''We managed to do that all on our own, didn't we?''

Anything else they might have said to one another was interrupted as Poppy and Gretchen rejoined them. ''Let's ride on another ride,'' Gretchen exclaimed, her cheeks pink with heightened excitement.

''You've got it, poppet,'' Travis said, and swung her up in his arms. ''And if I'm lucky, maybe I'll be able to win you a big stuffed animal before the day is over.''

Francine fought against a wave of guilt as she saw father and daughter together. Was she doing the right thing? Keeping the secret of Gretchen's birth from him? She shoved her doubts away, refusing to dwell on anything other than laughter and joy.

Travis couldn't remember when he'd had so much fun. Perhaps never in his life had he enjoyed such a special day. As they went from ride to ride, he watched Francine, remembering so many of the qualities that had initially drawn him to her. She'd always been a fascinating bundle of contradictions. Easy to offend, quick to strike back. Strong yet vulnerable, proud but needy.

She had a lust for life that he envied. She threw herself into each experience as if it might be her very last and she inspired in him a passion for life that he'd never felt with anyone else.

Even Poppy seemed to loosen up as the day wore on, laughing frequently and throwing himself into the fun. And, of course, there was Gretchen, who mirrored her mother, with her sparkling blue eyes and dark hair.

Something about the little girl tugged at Travis's heart. Perhaps it was the sweetness of her nature, the way she seemed to find something positive in everything and everyone. It would be a joy to raise such a child, to experience the world through her eyes.

Late in the afternoon, they all sat down at one of the tables in the concession area to eat an early dinner. "I want a chili dog and cotton candy," Gretchen said as Travis took everyone's orders

"Gretchen, you've already had three cotton-candy cones. Let's wait an hour or so before you get another one," Francine said.

"If you wait, I'll ride the Tilt-a-Whirl with you, then I'll eat a cotton candy with you," Poppy said.

"Just what we need," Francine said a moment later to Travis as the two of them went up to the counter to buy their meal, "a hyper little girl and a grouchy old man, both with sugar highs."

Travis laughed. "Poppy is quite taken with your daughter."

She looked back to the table, where the two sat together. "Yes, he is."

Travis saw the internal clouds that darkened her eyes and knew she was thinking of her own childhood with Poppy. "Sooner or later, Frannie, you're going to have to let it go," he said softly.

She looked at him in surprise. "What do you mean?"

He gestured with his head toward where Poppy and Gretchen had their heads together, whispering about something. "The fact that your daughter has managed to touch his heart like you never could."

He knew he'd voiced what she was thinking by the rueful smile that lifted one corner of her mouth. "You always did have an irritating habit of reading my mind," she said.

Her smile faded, and she looked back at Poppy and Gretchen. "Initially, I was worried that Poppy would somehow manage to inhibit Gretchen's natural exuberance, but somehow she's managed to imbue him with it." She shook her head. "It's nothing short of amazing."

"She's a special little girl."

Francine smiled fully, the gesture lighting her face with beauty. "Yes, she is. She's my heart."

And you're mine. The words nearly tumbled from his lips, stopped only by conscious effort. They lived in different worlds, had different dreams, and no confession of love from him would change that fact.

He couldn't stop her from chasing dreams, never wanted to be the reason she hadn't achieved those dreams. He didn't pretend to understand all the forces that had driven her away from Cooperville, but he knew he couldn't be the stumbling block in her plans.

Moments later, he and Francine returned to the table, bearing trays laden with food. "We'll probably all be sick," he observed as he passed out the chili-covered hot dogs, the greasy french fries and the sodas.

"Probably not as sick as that apple pie made you both years ago," Poppy replied, causing both Francine and Travis to look at him in surprise. "Or when you snuck behind the barn to try some of my pipe tobacco rolled up in newspaper.''

Francine gasped, and Travis laughed. ''I guess there wasn't much that got by you, Poppy,'' he exclaimed.

Poppy's eyes twinkled with a merry light. ''I figure I was twice as smart as both of you thought I was. Still am.''

They all laughed, then ate with the gusto of happiness.

It was late evening when they finally started home. Gretchen immediately curled up and fell sound asleep in the back seat, her head in Poppy's lap while her arms hugged the stuffed purple dinosaur Travis had won for her by throwing a ball at milk bottles. Poppy looked just as exhausted, his head leaned back against the seat with his eyes closed.

As Travis drove, his gaze alternated between the road and Frannie. Although her sundress was wrinkled and a spot of chili decorated the bodice, her hair was mussed and her makeup was worn off, she looked lovely.

He wished he was driving her back to their home, where he'd tuck Gretchen into bed, then take Frannie into his arms and make love to her until morning light sneaked in through the curtains.

He wished he'd eat his breakfast with Gretchen on one side of him and Francine on the other, their chatter permeating the silent corners of his house, filling up the empty spaces in his heart.

He frowned, disturbed by wishes that would never be fulfilled. Obviously, he had a streak of masochism hiding someplace inside him. That was the only way to explain him consciously choosing to spend the day in Frannie's company, knowing he'd never have a forever with her.

Maybe it was time he started dating. With his sisters raised, he had the time, although he'd never had the inclination. For the past five years, his heart had been mourning for the girl he'd loved and lost. Maybe it was time to get past the scars Francine had left behind.

"It was a nice day, wasn't it?" Francine said, breaking into his thoughts.

"Yes, it was," he agreed.

"I can't remember the last time I had so much fun."

He looked at her. "Surely you've had days to rival this one in the big city." He heard the edge to his voice, but didn't know how to control it.

Her gaze met his for a moment, and then she turned and looked out the passenger window. "Life in New York is not so much filled with fun as it is working to survive." Her voice was soft, as if she was reluctant to admit what she'd just said.

"But it's what you wanted," he reminded her.

Her head snapped around and she looked at him. "It still is," she said with fierce determination. "It's just that the past five years haven't been all fun and games."

"But you've attained a certain amount of success."

"I've barely been able to make a living," she replied. She looked into the back seat, apparently to assure herself that Poppy and Gretchen were asleep. "Travis, I came home because I was flat broke. I didn't know what else to do, where else to go."

He flashed her a look of surprise. "But the post-cards you sent Poppy made it sound like you were doing terrific. You had that part in the play, the stint in the soap opera."

She looked down at her hands, then stared at the dashboard. "Do you have any idea how expensive it is to live in New York? Not only did I have living expenses, but I also had a huge hospital bill to pay off when Gretchen was born."

"Her father didn't help financially?" The thought of Francine and Gretchen struggling to make ends meet pained him.

She shook her head. "Two acting jobs in five years isn't exactly the height of success." She straightened her shoulders. "But things will be different when we get back. Gretchen will be starting school, and that will give me more time and opportunity to audition."

He noticed the forward thrust of her jaw, a familiar gesture he'd always associated with her intense stubbornness. "I'm going to chase my happiness until I catch it," she said firmly, then added softly, "There are just times when I feel like I'm having to run too fast."

"I guess the important thing is that you stay focused on your dreams." It was a difficult thing for him to do, encouraging her to follow dreams that would only take her far away from him again.

He pulled up in front of the Webster house and shut off the engine. Travis turned in his seat and looked at the two in the back seat. Gretchen looked like a sleeping cherub and Poppy resembled a snoring gnome. "I'll carry Gretchen if you'll get Poppy," he said, attempting to get back the lightheartedness that had marked the day until moments before.

"How about I carry Gretchen and you wake up Poppy?" Francine returned with a teasing smile.

Poppy snorted himself awake and looked at them with bleary eyes. "What are you two looking at?" he demanded. "Ain't you ever seen an old man asleep before?"

Francine laughed as Travis got out of the car and opened the back door to reach in and take Gretchen from Poppy's lap.

The little girl curled up against his chest, her body warm and snuggly and smelling like sunshine and cotton candy. Her arms reached up to embrace his neck, her body limp with the utter trust that he'd take care and not drop her.

As Poppy got out of the car, Francine reached in and picked up the purple dinosaur from where it had fallen on the floor. Poppy unlocked the front door and flipped on the living room light as they entered the house.

"Here, I'll take her," Francine said, setting the dinosaur on the sofa and reaching out her arms for her daughter.

"I've got her. Just tell me where to tuck her in," he replied, unwilling to relinquish the sweet bundle just yet. He'd never known before that holding a sleeping child could make a heart swell, that breathing in the innocence of a child could be such a heady experience.

He'd tried to imagine before what it would be like to be a father, but he'd never felt it the way he did at this moment.

He followed Francine up the stairs to her room, where a cot was against one wall, a single bed against the opposite one. He knew immediately which bed

was Gretchen's, for the sheets on the cot were decorated with dancing bears and beribboned ducks.

He bent down and placed Gretchen on the cot. She
opened her eyes and smiled at him—a sweet smile
that tore straight into his heart. "Hi, Uncle Travis.
Did I fall asleep?"

"You sure did." He touched the tip of her nose
with his index finger. "And now you can go back to
sleep, because you're in your own little bed."

She sat up with a frown. "Where's my dinosaur?"
she asked.

"Downstairs. I'll go get it," Francine said, and disappeared from the room.

"You think maybe we should take off your shoes
and socks before you go to sleep?" Travis suggested.

Gretchen nodded. As he watched, she struggled to
get off her tennis shoes and socks, then fell back on
the cot, yawning deep and long. "We had fun today,
didn't we?"

"We sure did." Travis sat on the edge of the cot
and smoothed a strand of the little girl's hair away
from her face.

"Poppy had fun, too."

"Yes, I think he did," Travis agreed.

"I love carnivals," she said, her eyelids half closing with sleepiness.

"I do, too."

"And I love cotton candy." Her voice slurred the
words.

"So do I," Travis said with a smile.

"And I love you."

For a moment, Travis couldn't answer. It was impossible to talk, with his heart in his throat. He swal-

lowed hard around it. "And I love you," he whispered to the sleeping child.

He stood as Francine came into the room, carrying the stuffed animal. She smiled and shook her head ruefully. "I guess I took too long," she said.

Travis moved to the doorway and watched as Francine placed the dinosaur next to Gretchen, then pulled the sheet up to cover them both. She pressed a kiss against the child's forehead and stroked her cheek with a loving touch.

She was a good mother, Travis thought as he followed Francine down the stairs a moment later. Despite the fact that she'd had no mother for most of her life, she'd managed to tap into maternal instincts of her own.

"I guess Poppy went on to bed," she said when they reached the empty living room. "It used to drive me crazy that he never said good-night and would just disappear into his bedroom."

Travis smiled. "He lived a long time by himself before you came to stay with him, and the last five years he's been alone again."

She nodded. "You want some coffee? I could put on a pot."

"No, I'd better get home. I've got a few chores to take care of before calling it a night." It had been a good day, and the topping had been Gretchen's sweet utterance of love for him. He didn't want to risk messing it up by spending too much time alone with Francine and getting into another argument.

"I'll walk you out," she said.

Together they walked out into the late evening. The last of the sunset had faded into the night sky, as if the brilliant colors had been chased to the far reaches of the horizon by the night clouds moving in.

"Travis, thanks for today," she said as they approached his car. "I have a feeling Gretchen will never forget her first carnival experience."

"I enjoyed it, too." He opened the car door and looked at her curiously. "Have you decided how much longer you're going to stay?"

Wariness instantly swept over her face. "Why?"

"Don't worry, this isn't the beginning of a nasty conversation," he assured her. "I'm just curious, that's all."

The wariness fell away, and she frowned thoughtfully. "I'm figuring another week to ten days or so. I'd like to be back in the city no later than the first week of September, so I can get Gretchen settled in school."

He thought of her confession as they'd driven home, that things had been a little more difficult than she let on in her glowing postcards. What had really brought her back to Cooperville? Had it been the need to see her daughter and grandfather get acquainted, or had it been survival?

"When you get back, if you ever need anything, you know, a little financial help to keep Gretchen in a school, or just for a pair of shoes or whatever, call me, okay?" He had no idea why the offer had come so easily, only that he couldn't stand the thought of the two of them being broke and so far away. Of course, he knew she would never do it. She'd never been able to put pride aside and ask for what she needed.

Francine's eyes appeared to shine with an unnatural light, as if she were overwhelmed by his offer.

"Thank you," she said softly, and placed a hand on his arm.

For a long moment, they stood looking at each other. Travis wondered if she had any idea how much he loved her. Could she possibly see it in his eyes, know the depth of emotion she'd always inspired in him?

Somehow he didn't think so. She'd always been very good at seeing only what she wanted, what she needed, to see. His love would only be a burden to her.

"I'll see you later," he said, and got into the car.

As he drove the short distance to his house, he wondered if Francine would ever have come home had she been as successful as she initially pretended? Somehow it disappointed him that need had brought her back, not desire.

He thought of his decision to start dating, the very idea filling him with dread. He couldn't imagine spending time with another woman, kissing lips other than Frannie's. However, he knew that unless he wanted to spend the rest of his life alone, he'd better get over this particular aversion. He had to get over Francine.

Pulling into his driveway, he realized it wasn't only Francine he would miss when they were gone. Gretchen had managed to burrow deep into his heart, lodging there like a tick beneath a dog's fur.

He shut off the car engine, but remained in the car, thinking of those moments when the little girl had snuggled against his heart. Three words. So simple. *I love you*. Three words with the power to build monuments, destroy civilizations and make a simple man want to cry.

Chapter Eight

She had had the dream again, only this time with a disturbing twist. As before, she'd stood onstage and the audience screamed her name over and over again. She reveled in their adulation, glowed beneath the waves of love that cascaded over her. That was when the dream changed.

The audience had faded, not even an echo of their adoring cries remaining. The spotlight had blinded her, shining with a heat that was too intense. She had shielded her gaze, attempting to see out into the darkened theater. Nothing. She had been alone. Desperately. Achingly. Alone.

"Frannie." The deep voice had come from the darkness in front of her. "Frannie." A sweet, familiar voice that had evoked a warmth that suffused her, a warmth as evocative, as comforting, as the one she'd felt at the crowd's cheers.

She'd awakened moments earlier, but she remained

still, trying to ignore the crazy implications of the dream. She didn't want to examine too closely why Travis's vocalizing her name filled her up as completely as an audience's admiration.

She rolled over on her side and looked at the clock, surprised to discover it was almost ten. She'd overslept. There was nothing she hated more than wasting a morning by sleeping it away, especially one of those rare mornings when she didn't have to be at the diner at the crack of dawn.

It took her only a few minutes to shower and dress, and then she went downstairs in search of Gretchen and Poppy. A note on the kitchen table told her that they'd gone into town for some shopping.

She poured herself the last cup of coffee left in the pot, then sat down at the kitchen table. As she replayed the day before in her mind, a smile lifted her lips. She'd had a wonderful time, and she knew Gretchen would always remember her very first carnival.

What she hoped Gretchen would forget was whispering her final words to Travis as sleep had overtaken her. Francine had just come up the stairs and been about to enter the bedroom when she heard her daughter tell Travis she loved him.

It had broken Francine's heart, and all the doubts she'd ever entertained about not telling Travis the truth had come back to haunt her.

Had she been wrong to keep Gretchen's birth a secret? No, she refused to consider her decision, made so long ago, a mistake. Although Travis's circumstances had changed and he was no longer surrounded by needy people, hers hadn't. She still wanted, needed, what New York and the stage could offer her.

She hadn't been wrong to keep Gretchen's birth from Travis. Her silence had been best for all involved, she told herself firmly.

She had finished her coffee and was washing out her cup when Travis walked in the back door. "Good morning," he said. "Where's Poppy? The garage door is up, but I didn't see his truck."

"He and Gretchen went into town," she replied. "Want some coffee? I could put on a fresh pot."

"No, I'm here for two specific purposes. First, I need to borrow a couple of tools from Poppy. My tractor is having a bad day, and I'm hoping a few adjustments will fix the problem."

"Help yourself to whatever you need in the shed. You know Poppy won't mind."

"The other reason I'm here is because Margaret called this morning. She's planning on coming home this afternoon for a quick visit, and insisted on a barbecue. I thought it would be nice if the three of you join us. She'd love to see you again, and meet Gretchen."

Francine hesitated. He looked so handsome this morning, clad in his jeans and a gray T-shirt. A streak of dirt or oil decorated his cheek, but that only added to his masculine attractiveness.

"I'm barbecuing my famous ribs," he added, as if to bribe her into coming.

She laughed. "I didn't know you had famous ribs."

"Won first prize the last three years at the county

fair." His cheeks flushed slightly with pride. "My secret sauce is the most coveted recipe in town."

"How can I say no? What time should we come, and what shall I bring?" Francine fought the impulse to reach out and swipe the streak from his cheek. She knew his skin would be warm and smooth beneath her fingertips.

"About three, and nothing. Susie's bringing dessert, and I'll provide the rest."

"We'll be there," she agreed, and he started back to the door.

"Tell Poppet the kittens can't wait to meet her," he said, then left.

She stood in the doorway and watched as he walked toward the shed where Poppy kept his tools. He had the walk of a man confident about himself, content with his life.

He's happy, she thought with a kind of wonder. He's happy being a farmer, working with the land and living a small-town life.

For the first time, she realized Travis would have never been happy in New York City. Had he come with her so many years before, little pieces of his soul would have died.

She'd always known their dreams were different, but she'd consciously refused to think about the consequences of those different aspirations. At the time she left Cooperville, there'd still been pieces of a hurt little girl inside, a little girl who needed to know Travis would love her more than anything else on earth, more than duty, more than family, more than himself. She'd been wrong to expect that.

How could she blame him for following his heart,

when that was exactly what she had done? And with that thought, a sense of peace descended over her, a final forgiveness that banished any lingering bitterness she'd held in her heart for him.

As she remained at the door, Travis exited the shed, carrying several tools.

She loved him. Yesterday. Today. Always.

The emotion struck her like a slap to the face, stealing her breath and making her lean weakly against the screen door.

She'd thought what she felt for him was simply the old memories of past love, that she'd moved beyond loving Travis.

As she watched him walk away, she realized that without her bitterness there was nothing to stop the love that flowed into her heart for him.

She also realized something else. Somewhere in the space of the past five years, her dreams had changed. She'd come to realize that New York didn't hold the happiness she craved. Stardom would never be enough to fill the heart of a little girl who'd never felt loved.

That was what her dream had been telling her the night before. She'd believed an audience's roar could take away her emptiness, but it couldn't. Only when Travis whispered her name so sweet, so lovingly, did the emptiness fill with warmth.

She turned away from the door, her heart heavy with sadness. But it didn't matter how much she loved Travis. He'd never indicated that those feelings were reciprocated.

The crunch of gravel and a familiar engine backfire

announced Poppy and Gretchen's return. Francine stepped out onto the porch to greet them.

The moment the truck pulled to a halt, Gretchen scrambled from the passenger seat. "Mommy, look what Poppy got me!" She struck a pose to show off the miniature overalls she wore. "They're just like the ones Poppy and Uncle Travis wear," she exclaimed proudly.

"They certainly are," Francine replied.

"Now I'm a real farm girl," Gretchen said, hooking her thumbs in her straps the way Poppy often did.

"I figured overalls are practical for chores," Poppy said, as if his sole reason for buying them were pragmatic, rather than to see the delighted shine in Gretchen's eyes. "Speaking of chores." He eyed the little girl sternly. "Did you take care of the rabbits this morning?"

"I'll go do it right now," Gretchen said, and headed down the dirt path.

"Take that dog with you," Poppy yelled after her. "She could use a good run."

Gretchen stopped and unchained Beauty, who pranced and barked in excitement. Together, the two disappeared down the path.

"You shouldn't let her talk you into buying her things," Francine said as she and Poppy headed inside.

"She didn't talk me into anything," he protested. "The overalls was my idea." He looked at her with a touch of defiance. "I reckon I can buy my great-granddaughter something without having to explain myself."

"I reckon you can," Francine agreed with a smile.

Poppy seemed to relax, as if he'd geared himself up for a fight that didn't come. He sat at the kitchen table and drew a deep breath. "I will say this…that little Miss Beans could talk a man to death without any trouble."

Francine laughed. "She is rather sociable. Speaking of being sociable, we've been invited to a barbecue this afternoon at Travis's."

"He making ribs?" Poppy asked. Francine nodded. Poppy almost smiled. "Good. Travis is the best rib cooker around these parts."

"That's exactly what he told me."

This time Poppy did smile. "He's a good man, Frannie. A woman could do a lot worse than Travis."

Francine felt her heart ache at his words. "I know," she answered softly. "But a woman has to want what it is he offers for it to be right."

For a long moment, Poppy stared at her. Then he snorted and stood. "I think I'll take me a little walk. I've never suffered fools very well."

Francine stared after him as he banged out of the door. Was she a fool? Was there a possibility for happiness here with Travis?

For the first time, she considered the likelihood of it. Was fate giving them a second chance to find a forever together? She closed her eyes, for a moment able to imagine what it would be like, waking in his arms each morning, sleeping beside him every night. Heaven. The stuff of dreams.

Maybe, just maybe, it was time for Francine to chase the dream she really wanted to come true. Just maybe it was time she told Travis of her new dream.

* * *

"Francine, gosh, you look exactly like you did five years ago!" Margaret exclaimed as she hugged Francine.

Francine laughed. "I wish I could say the same thing about you." She stepped back and eyed the young girl with genuine affection. "Last time I saw you, you were a thirteen-year-old with braces and a bad haircut you'd given yourself."

Margaret laughed and nodded her head. "Oh, gosh, I'd nearly forgotten that haircut." She bent down to introduce herself to Gretchen. "Hi, I'm Margaret, Travis's baby sister."

Gretchen giggled. "You don't look like a baby to me," she exclaimed.

"We going to stand around all day jawing, or are we going to get comfortable?" Poppy exclaimed.

Margaret laughed and, to Francine's surprise, kissed Poppy on the cheek. "Come on, Poppy, I've got your favorite lawn chair set up." She winked at Francine and linked arms with the old man. "Travis is waiting for us in the backyard."

Together they all walked around the side of the house to the back, where Travis, clad in overalls and a checkered apron, stood in front of a smoking brick barbecue pit.

He waved a pair of tongs in their direction and flashed a smile that could have melted a snowdrift.

"Uncle Travis," Gretchen said. "Look, I have overalls just like yours." She raced over to him, eager to show off her farm attire. Poppy followed, dragging his lawn chair closer to where Travis was working.

"She's a doll," Margaret said.

"Thanks. I'm pretty partial to her," Francine replied with a smile. She looked at the pretty, dark-haired young woman. "I understand you're about to start classes at the University of Nebraska."

"Classes start in two weeks." Margaret gestured toward the picnic table, and they both sat down. "But I've been there for a little over a month. I'm not staying in a dorm. My best friend and I are sharing an apartment, so we went early to get settled in and find part-time jobs."

"Sounds like fun," Francine said.

"It is." Her gaze went to Travis. "Although I miss Travis and Susie. Thank goodness I'm close enough and have a schedule that should allow me to get home at least twice a month."

"That's nice. It's always difficult to be away from home." Francine remembered all too well the nights of homesickness she'd suffered when she first left.

"Yeah." Margaret smiled, and again her gaze shot to her brother. "Although Travis would never admit it, I think he's suffering empty-nest syndrome."

"What makes you think so?" Francine asked curiously.

"Oh, I don't know. Sometimes when I talk to him on the phone, he just sounds so lonely. I wish he'd find some nice woman, get married and fill this old house with babies." She looked at Francine, her gaze filled with warmth. "There was a time when I was certain that woman would be you." She touched Francine's hand. "I always liked the idea of you being my sister-in-law."

A lump the size of a Nebraska sunflower filled Francine's throat. Before she could reply, Susie and her husband appeared, and Francine was swept up in a new round of hugs and introductions.

The afternoon went quickly, the hours consumed by laughter, eating and memories. Francine was struck not only by how delightful Travis's sisters were, but also by the obvious love and respect they felt for Travis.

Francine wondered how her life might have been different if she had a family, loving parents and siblings. Would her choices have been different if she basked in love, and not hungered beneath Poppy's stern disapproval?

She envied Travis what he had here. While she struggled to make ends meet, seeking elusive stardom, he'd built a family...and she wanted desperately to be a part of it. She wanted it not only for herself, but for Gretchen, as well.

"You're looking quite thoughtful," Susie said as she slid onto the picnic bench next to Francine. They had cleared up the dinner mess and put away the leftovers. Moments earlier, Travis had set up a croquet course, and everyone except Susie and Francine was playing.

"Just enjoying the evening," Francine replied.

"There's nothing better than a day spent with family," Susie said.

Francine smiled. "And I understand your family is about to expand. Congratulations."

"Thanks." Susie's face glowed. "We're really excited about it." She touched her stomach, as if caressing the baby growing within. "Richard and I are hoping to have lots of children." She looked over at her husband, a handsome young man who appeared to believe she'd hung the moon.

"Richard seems like a nice guy," Francine observed.

Again Susie's face lit with a glow. "He's more than that. He's my soul mate."

Soul mate. Had Travis been her soul mate? She looked over to where Travis was playing croquet, laughing as he sent Poppy's ball to the outer reaches of the court. Yes, he'd been her soul mate, and she couldn't imagine how she'd summoned up the stupidity to walk away from him.

A simple man, yes. He'd never needed much to make him happy. She remembered now the nights when she'd lain in his arms and he'd talked to her of his dreams...dreams that included barbecues and family, the desire for a wife and children.

Could she embrace his dream as her own? Leave behind her aspirations of fame and stardom? He hadn't loved her enough to stop her from leaving years ago. In the past several weeks, had his feelings for her deepened? Was it possible that if she remained here long enough, he'd grow to love her enough to want to spend the rest of his life with her? In order to find out, she would have to put her pride on the line, and that had never been easy for Francine.

As evening fell, casting purple shadows that made it impossible to play the game, they all gathered on the back porch for homemade ice cream and cake.

"This is yummy," Gretchen said as she finished the last of her ice cream and held out her bowl for more.

"There's nothing better than homemade ice cream

on a hot summer night,'' Travis said as he dipped her some more. When he'd filled her bowl once again, Gretchen climbed up on his lap as if it were the most natural thing in the world.

Francine's heart convulsed at the sight of father and daughter, so obviously taken with each other. Was it possible that what they felt for each other was the unconscious pull of shared genes? Although their minds had no idea of their connection, was it possible their hearts felt it?

''There's only one more thing that would make this an utterly perfect night,'' Susie said as she looked at her big brother. ''Would you get out the guitar and sing a couple songs?''

''I don't think that's necessary,'' Travis protested.

''Please, Uncle Travis,'' Gretchen said, apparently delighted at the idea. ''I can sing, too. We could sing together.''

Travis smiled at the little girl, his heart in his eyes for all of them to see. ''I can't say no to you, little poppet.'' As Gretchen climbed off his lap, he stood and went into the house. He reappeared a moment later with his guitar.

He sat back down on the chair, and Gretchen sank down at his feet, her bowl of ice cream forgotten as she watched him strum the strings to produce sweet, melodic sound.

Francine leaned her head back against her chair as his fingers evoked harmony from the instrument. The night insects quieted, as if enjoying the sweet tones of music that filled the air.

Gretchen moved closer and leaned her head against

Travis's knee, her gaze adoring him and creating a myriad of emotions in Francine's heart.

She'd always believed she could be enough for Gretchen, that she had a deep enough well of love for her daughter inside her to fill the absence of a father in the little girl's life. She realized now that she'd been wrong.

As Travis began to sing an old ballad, Francine allowed his deep, dulcet voice to flow over her. There had been a time when she believed Travis had the ability to sing himself to prominence. She'd believed his voice would be his ticket to stardom, while her acting ability would be hers.

Now she realized he'd been right all along. As she watched her daughter listen to him sing, she knew his voice was meant for lullabies.

Somehow, in the space of the past couple of weeks, his dreams had become more appealing than her own. After a day spent in the company of his sisters, feeling the love that existed between them, she realized he'd achieved a kind of stardom in his own right, one much more long-lasting than any she'd ever tried to attain.

It was after ten when Margaret got into her car to travel back to school, and by that time Francine had come to the decision that before the night was over, she was going to bare her heart and soul to Travis. It was time to see if fate would give them one last chance to find happiness together.

Susie and Richard were next to leave, kissing everyone warmly before getting into their car and driving off. Travis disappeared into the house, carrying dessert bowls and coffee cups to the kitchen.

"I think Miss Beans is ready to call it a night, too," Poppy said to Francine, gesturing toward where Gretchen sat in a lounge chair, fighting off sleep.

"Would you mind taking her on home? I'll stay and help Travis with the last of the cleanup, then walk back home," she said.

Poppy studied her for a long moment. "It's about time," he said. "Time you told that boy about his daughter." Francine stared at him in surprise. He snorted and shook his head ruefully. "I'm not the old fool you take me for, although I was beginning to wonder how long you were going to be a young fool." He turned and called to Gretchen.

Francine stared after the car as Poppy drove Gretchen back to the house. The taillights remained visible all the way, not blinking off until Poppy parked in front of his house and shut off the car engine.

So, Poppy had known all along that Gretchen was Travis's daughter. He hadn't been fooled by her fudging Gretchen's age. She smiled and shook her head ruefully. Apparently Poppy hadn't lied when he said not much got by him.

She could hear Travis's happy whistle drifting out the back door as he rattled plates and ran water in the sink. Surely he'd be happy when she told him. He'd obviously grown very fond of Gretchen over the past couple of weeks.

For the first time, fear rippled through her as she thought of confessing to Travis. Would he be happy to learn the news? Would they get a second chance to find happiness together? Did her future lie with Travis, here in Cooperville?

Funny, five years ago she couldn't imagine making a life here. But since her return, the town and its people had embraced her as if she were a prodigal daughter returned. Since coming back, she'd felt a sense of belonging she'd never experienced before.

Thoughts of going back to New York no longer held any appeal. The only stars she was interested in were the ones she hoped would shine from Travis's eyes.

Was her future here? There was only one way to find out. Drawing a deep breath, she opened the back door and stepped into the kitchen.

Chapter Nine

It had been the kind of day Travis loved, a day of family and friends, of laughter and warmth. His heart was filled to the top with happiness.

It worried him more than a little bit to contemplate what his life would be like when Francine and Gretchen returned to New York. He hadn't realized his life had such voids in it until they came home and filled those spaces up.

He hadn't noticed the emptiness so much when he was busy raising Margaret and Susie, but in the time since Susie married and Margaret left home, there had been an abiding loneliness that even his visits with Poppy couldn't assuage.

He turned as the back door opened and flashed a smile at Francine. "Where's everyone else?" he asked.

"Gone. Poppy took one tired little girl home. I decided it was only fair I stick around and help with the cleanup, since you did all the cooking."

"Good. I hate rinsing dishes and loading the dishwasher." He dried his hands, gave her the sponge, then sat down at the kitchen table and gestured her toward the sink.

Francine laughed. "I'd expected a little more of a fight," she said as she took over the task.

"Not when it comes to that," he replied. He leaned back in the chair, pleased she had decided to stay. "It was a great day, wasn't it?" he asked, wondering if she'd felt the same magic of togetherness that he had.

"Yes, it was," she agreed.

"How about a cup of coffee?" he asked as he stood. "It will just take a jiffy to make a fresh pot." He wanted her to stay, he wanted them to sit together at the table and talk about the day as if they were a long-married couple. He wanted the illusion of magic to continue.

"Coffee sounds good."

Within minutes, the coffee was gurgling as it drained into the glass carafe, the hearty scent filling the kitchen. Francine placed the last bowl in the dishwasher as Travis poured them each a cup of the fresh brew.

"Why don't we take it back out to the porch?" he suggested. "I hate to waste a beautiful night."

He led the way, and together they sat on the porch swing. He was overly conscious of the warmth of her bare thigh as it pressed against his, radiating through the denim of his overalls. The scent of her perfume eddied in the air, as fragrant as any sweet-smelling flower, and he fought against a wave of desire that nearly stole his breath away.

He watched her as she sipped her coffee, then tilted

her gaze upward toward the night sky. "I think the stars hang lower in Nebraska than in any other place on earth," she said softly.

He smiled. "Remember when we were young and believed fireflies were flashing stars that had fallen from the sky?"

She laughed, the sound twisting his heart into a knot. "Oh, my, I'd forgotten that." She sighed. "You can rarely see the stars in New York City. All the lights and the smog make you believe the stars have disappeared forever."

Stay here. His heart longed to say the words. *Stay here where the stars are always in the heavens. Stay here and be a part of my life.* He bit his tongue, then took a drink of his coffee, not giving the words a chance to sneak out.

There was nothing to be gained by baring his heart. He knew she'd go back to New York, back to chasing the dreams that had driven her for most of her life…the dreams that would always be between them.

He shoved these thoughts away, refusing to dwell on the unhappy circumstances he couldn't change. At the moment, he simply wanted to enjoy this time with her, with no bitter recriminations from the past and no haunting visions of a future without her.

He placed an arm around her back, and she leaned into him, just as she had a thousand times before, a lifetime ago. There was nothing sexual about their closeness, only an abiding contentment, built on trust and the deep bonds of friendship.

"Margaret and Susie are lovely, Travis. You did a wonderful job with them," she said.

He smiled as a wistful ache filled his heart. "I'm

only sorry Mom isn't here to see them. She would have been so proud to see the women they've become.'' He tightened his arm around her shoulders. ''Just as I know your mother would be proud of the woman you've become.''

She sighed again—a sweet whisper of breath against his neck. ''I wish I remembered my parents better,'' she said. ''It used to scare me that with each day that passed my memories of them got weaker and weaker, until one day I could barely remember what they looked like. Then there was a time when I was glad I didn't remember them, because I was so mad at them.''

''Mad?'' Travis looked at her in surprise.

''They left me. That's the way it felt.'' She shook her head with a rueful smile. ''I know it's irrational, but I was so angry, not only because they'd gone away and never come back, but they'd left me with a man who was incapable of loving me.''

She was silent a moment, then continued. ''Poppy never talked about them. We never mentioned their existence, in all the years I lived with him.''

Travis kept quiet, knowing instinctively that this was something she needed to talk about, but intrigued with this new facet to her personality, a piece of herself that she'd never gifted him with before.

In all their years of friendship, of devotion to one another, she'd never talked about her parents at all. That had been the one topic that he always knew was off-limits.

''Tell me what you do remember about them,'' he urged.

She sat up and once again looked up at the stars.

"Little, inconsequential things, that's what I remember. Like the smell of my mother's favorite perfume, and the way her hand felt when she stroked my forehead. I remember my dad's laughter. He had a loud, booming laugh that I adored."

She looked at Travis, the blue of her eyes darkened by an emotion he couldn't fathom. Apprehension? Fear? "Frannie...what is it?" he asked.

She finished the last of her coffee, then set the mug on the porch. "Growing up without a parent always leaves a hole, doesn't it?"

Travis thought of his own father, who'd passed away when he was fifteen, and then the loss of his mother, when he was twenty-two. Both deaths had definitely left behind an emptiness that was difficult to fill. "Yes, but things happen. People die."

"But it would be a terrible thing, to keep a child and a parent away from each other if both were alive," she said.

Travis felt a strange discomfort flood him. Where was she going with this? What was going on in that brain of hers? "Francine, what are you getting at?"

She stood and moved to the porch railing, her back to him. He could see her tension in the rigid lines of her body, and an answering anxiety built up within him.

"Talk to me, Francine," he said as he leaned over and set his cup on the porch next to hers.

She turned to face him, but her gaze didn't meet his. Instead, she stared just over his shoulder, as if finding it impossible to look into his eyes. "Gretchen is your daughter, Travis."

It was as if she'd spoken in a foreign language. For

a moment, her words made no sense, and he struggled to fit them into his reality.

Gretchen was his? How was that possible? What was Francine trying to do? He swallowed, fighting a myriad of emotions. "What do you mean?" he asked, his voice sounding strained and harsh to his own ears.

"She's not three years old. She's four. She was conceived the night before I left for New York." Her gaze met his. "She's your daughter, Travis."

Joy welled up in his heart. The poppet was his...his daughter, his little girl. No wonder he'd felt such a connection with her, despite his reluctance to the contrary.

Instantly, anger squashed the joy, an anger that tightened his chest as he realized how much of Gretchen's childhood he'd lost.

No...not lost. It had been taken. Stolen by Francine.

He stood and walked toward Francine, stopping when he was mere inches from where she stood. "How could you? How could you have kept this from me all this time?"

Her features twisted with sorrow, and she held out her hands to him in supplication. "Travis, I was already in New York when I realized I was pregnant."

"Why didn't you call me? Write and tell me? I had a right to know." The words exploded out of him, and she cringed beneath their accusation. He took a step back from her, his heart aching.

She drew herself up and sucked in a deep breath. "You're right. You had a right to know, but at the time there were several reasons why I didn't tell you."

"What possible reason could you have had?" he demanded.

Once again her gaze shifted from his, as if she were unable to speak while looking into his eyes. "You've always been an honorable man, Travis. I knew you'd insist we do the right thing, get married. At that time, you were caring for your mother and trying to raise your two sisters. The last thing you needed was another responsibility...two more burdens."

"And you knew I'd insist you come back here," he added bitterly. "You would have had to give up your dreams."

She nodded her head slightly, as if the thought caused her pain. At least she didn't deny it. "Maybe that played into it. I'm not sure anymore."

For a long moment, neither of them said a word. She remained at the railing, looking defeated and weary and he fought the profound anger that still flowed through him, an anger mixed with the heady high of jubilation.

Gretchen was his. Born with his genes, a continuity of his family line. She was a child not only of his body, but of his heart.

"Travis...I'm sorry," Francine whispered and placed a hand on his arm.

He shook off her touch. "Sorry?" His heart constricted with sorrow. "Do you have any idea what you've robbed me of? I'll never hold her as a newborn in my arms. I'll never see her first step. Moment after precious moment of her childhood has already been lost forever to me."

A sob tore from her throat and tears glistened in her eyes, but Travis remained unmoved by her emotion, too filled with his own. "Travis, I was trying to do what was best for everyone, because I loved you."

Travis laughed. It was a harsh, bitter sound. "Love? Francine, you have no idea what that word means." Tears of his own blurred his vision, and he stumbled back another step from her, needing some distance, needing time to assess what he'd just learned.

"Don't you see what you've done?" he asked, his tone incredulous. "How could you have spent all those years with me and not know how important this would be to me? Night after night you listened to my dreams of having a family, being a father."

Once again emotion filled him, so thick, so heavy, he couldn't speak. He swallowed against it, blinking to dispel any lingering tears. "You had my dream right in your hand for the last five years, and you kept it away from me. That's not love, Francine." He paused a moment, then continued. "And I don't know if I can ever forgive you for that."

"I'm sorry," she said softly. She hesitated a moment, as if to add something else, then walked off the porch and disappeared into the darkness of the night.

She should have never told him. Minutes later, as she sat in the darkness at her bedroom window, tears oozing down her cheeks, she cursed herself for telling him.

She'd hoped that tonight she would become a part of his life, that somehow they'd put the past behind them and begin to build a future together. She'd been a fool.

And now she needed to decide exactly where her

future was, whether she should remain here in Cooperville or go back to New York.

"And I don't know if I can forgive you for that." Travis's words echoed in her head, squeezing her heart painfully. How could she stay here and see him every day, watch him as he dated other women, perhaps married? How could she watch him build a life that didn't include her and not die just a little bit? Without Travis, what was left for her here?

It would be better if she went back to New York, continued to pursue the dreams that had once motivated her, sustained her. She could build a life there just as easily as she could build one here. And there she would not have to see Travis, wouldn't have to feel the weight of his disappointment, his bitterness, his hatred toward her.

By the time dawn lit the eastern sky, she'd made up her mind. There was nothing for her here. Poppy had never cared much for her, and now she didn't even have Travis's love to balance the old man's antipathy. Perhaps she could find some sort of happiness in New York City.

Although she would have liked to stay several weeks longer to add to the nest egg in the dresser drawer, she decided it was best to leave first thing in the morning. That would give her today to pack, and hopefully the night to get a good night's sleep.

Decision made, she crept down to the kitchen to make coffee, knowing any sleep would be impossible right now. She carried a cup of the fresh brew out on to the porch, wanting to see her last Nebraska sunrise.

As she watched the colors splash across the sky, her heartache expanded in her chest. She suspected now that what had brought her back here was the ridiculous hope that she and Travis could pick up where they'd left off years before. The joy and utter fulfillment of being held in his arms had never been replaced by any other experience in her life.

He'd been right. She had stolen his dream from him. Regret welled up inside her as she once again replayed his parting words in her mind. She'd always known how important children were, how much of a role being a father played in his dreams.

She had been selfish...and afraid. She'd been afraid he would want Gretchen, that somehow she would be left with nothing. And from the moment of her birth, Gretchen had been the one person in Frannie's life who offered her unconditional love, total commitment.

Foolishly, she hadn't considered that in keeping Gretchen away from Travis, she was depriving her daughter of a very important relationship, the love of a special daddy. She had to acknowledge that, selfishly, she hadn't wanted to share her daughter with anyone. She'd been afraid that sharing Gretchen would mean less love for her.

How easy it was to see the error of your ways when it was too late to fix things. Her gaze drifted from the splendid sunrise to Travis's house.

He hated her. She'd seen it glittering from his eyes. Nothing would ever be able to change what she'd done. However, she could allay some of the damage by giving him time with Gretchen. When she got back to New York, she would write him, work out some sort of custody agreement.

They would deal with this issue as if they were a

divorced couple. Gretchen could spend several weeks during the summer and occasional holidays here with Travis. Surely Francine and Travis could come to a civil agreement, so that both of them would have roles in Gretchen's life. Roles in Gretchen's life. It sounded so cold...so utterly civil.

She finished her coffee and went back into the kitchen, surprised to see Poppy seated at the table. "I didn't hear you get up," she said as she rinsed her cup in the sink.

"I've been awake for some time. I didn't sleep very well."

"There must be an epidemic of that going around," Francine answered dryly. She returned her cup to the cabinet, then turned back to face him. He looked unusually old, tired, this morning, and for a moment she was reluctant to say anything to him. But he'd have to know sooner or later what her plans were, and it was better that she tell him now. "Gretchen and I will be leaving in the morning."

He looked at her in surprise. "Why?"

Francine shrugged. "It's time we get back to our own lives."

"Did you tell Travis about Miss Beans?"

"I told him," she answered succinctly.

Poppy's eyebrows drew together in an unbroken fuzzy line across his brow. "And he's going to let you take her away?"

Francine flushed with a stir of anger. "He has no choice in this matter. She's my daughter, and she goes where I go."

"He's her father." Poppy rubbed his chest, as if he had an irritating itch.

"And I'll make sure he gets an opportunity to see her, spend time with her," Francine replied. "I'll see to it that she comes back here for occasional visits."

He got up from the table and went to the sink. He got a glass of water and drank it as Francine fought back tears. What was wrong with her? Leaving was the right decision, the best decision. So why did she have such a painful knot in her heart? She was just overtired, she told herself.

Poppy finished his water and turned to her, his eyes filled with a sadness that only made the knot in her chest grow larger. "Miss Beans won't want to leave."

"She's a child, she doesn't know what's best," Francine answered.

"Ain't no kind of a life for a child." Poppy slammed his glass down on the counter with unnatural force. "Living in a big city full of concrete and noise. Ain't no kind of a life at all."

"Lots of children are raised in New York City, and they grow up to be happy, well-adjusted adults." Poppy snorted, and Francine felt her anger rise. "Don't make this more difficult for me than it already is. I can't stay here. I can't be happy here."

Poppy was silent. As he had been so many times in her past. It was a silence that grew, expanded and filled with the weight of his disappointment. Disappointment. Never love.

Always before, Francine had suffered his silences stoically, long resigned to the fact that he would never love her, never even like her very much. But this time, his oppressive silence caused something to snap inside her.

"I know you don't want me here," she said, her voice unsteady with suppressed tears. "I find it nothing short of amazing that you've somehow managed to love Gretchen, when you could never love me."

"Don't be guessing what I feel and don't feel!" he exclaimed.

"I don't have to guess," Francine said, her voice rising as old emotions and bitterness cascaded through her. "I lived it. I lived with your silences and your coldness. I lived every day knowing you didn't want me here, but there was no place else for me to go, nobody else who wanted me."

Hot tears streaked her cheeks as all her old hurts, all the childish feelings of being unloved, rose to the surface.

"Francine…"

She held up her hand, not wanting to hear anything he had to say. Any words of comfort he might have to offer would only be lies. And at least until this moment in time, he'd never resorted to lies with her.

"Gretchen and I are leaving tomorrow morning, and nothing you can say is going to change that fact." Without waiting for his reply, she stormed out the back door, the screen slamming behind her as she raced for the cornfield.

Once in the cover of the cornfield, she dropped to the ground, racked by sobs that had been pent up for far too long.

All those tears she'd refused to shed in childhood now flowed freely. For the first time, she grieved for her parents, lost to her through a tragic car accident. She cried for the little girl she'd been, who desperately needed love from an old man who offered none.

Finally, she cried for the woman she'd become. She'd finally traded her dreams for Travis's, hoping she could become a part of the life he'd achieved. But it was too late for her...too late for them.

For the very first time, she felt empty, completely devoid of warmth and life. Always before, she'd had her dreams to sustain her, but now they were gone, and Travis was gone.

She didn't know how long she remained hidden in the corn crop, allowing old wounds and new ones to possess her.

Finally, she swiped the last of the tears away, seeking within to find the strength that had always been hers. She would cry no more. Enough tears had been spent on things that couldn't be changed. It was time to move forward. Time to pack and prepare for the trip.

She stood and started to walk back. She was half-way between the cornfield and the house when Gretchen appeared at the back door, clad in her pajamas.

"Mommy...something is wrong with Poppy!" the little girl cried out. "He's sleeping on the kitchen floor and he won't wake up!"

Fear rippled through Francine as she had a sudden vision of Poppy rubbing his chest. For a moment, it felt as if her heart had stopped. "Oh, no!" she gasped and raced to the back door. She burst into the kitchen, her gaze instantly going to Poppy.

Sprawled on the floor, his face the color of gray paste, he lay unmoving. "Poppy!" she cried, and fell to the floor beside him.

"Mommy?" Gretchen's voice was thick with fear.

"It's going to be all right, honey," Francine said as she quickly loosened Poppy's shirt and maneuvered him into position for CPR. He looked so still, so frighteningly still. "I need you to be a big girl and call Uncle Travis. Tell him Poppy is sick and he needs to come right over."

Gretchen ran to the phone and picked up the receiver. As Francine told her the number, she carefully dialed. As Gretchen relayed the message to Travis, Francine began CPR, hoping...praying her confrontation with him hadn't killed him.

Chapter Ten

"Susie is on her way to get Gretchen," Travis said as he sat down next to Francine in the hospital waiting area. Francine nodded absently, her gaze going to her daughter, who was still clad in her pajamas, stretched out on the floor thumbing through a children's book.

The past hour had been a nightmare. By the time Travis arrived at the house, Poppy had been breathing, but still unconscious. They'd carried him to the car, placed him in the back seat, then driven like the wind to get him to the nearest hospital.

Within minutes of arriving at the hospital, Poppy had been whisked away, and they had been sent to wait...and wait...and wait.

"Why doesn't somebody come out here and tell us what's going on?" Francine asked. She stood, too frantic to remain seated. "What can be taking so long?"

"I'm sure somebody will come out and tell us

something as soon as they have something to tell us,"
Travis said as she paced back and forth in front of
him.

"Mommy?" Gretchen closed her book and got up
from the floor. "Is Poppy going to be okay?"

Francine picked up her daughter. Like a baby mon-
key, Gretchen wrapped her legs around her mother's
waist. "I'm sure Poppy is going to be just fine.
Heaven won't take him and hell can't handle him,"
she added wryly, praying her words would prove true.

Gretchen's eyes widened. "Mommy, you said a
bad word."

"I'll wash her mouth out with soap later," Travis
remarked.

Gretchen giggled and scrambled down from Francine's arms. She picked the book up off the floor and
went over to Travis. "Would you read this to me?"
she asked.

"Sure." Travis pulled the little girl up onto his lap.

As Travis began to read the storybook to Gretchen,
Francine once again paced the confines of the small
waiting room.

Guilt ripped through her as she thought of that horrifying moment of discovering Poppy on the floor.
She should never have fought with him. She should
never have allowed her emotions to fly so out of control.

She would never forgive herself if something happened to Poppy. She would never forgive herself if
he died before she had a chance to tell him how much
she loved him.

She stopped in her tracks as Dr. Carterson entered
the waiting room. Instantly Travis was at her side, his

hand cupping her elbow, as if he intended to support her throughout any bad news.

In some portion of her mind, she was thankful. Despite their differences, in spite of his negative feelings toward her, it was comforting to know that in this, they were simply two people who loved Poppy.

"He's resting easy for the moment," Dr. Carterson said. A sob of relief escaped Francine, and she leaned weakly against Travis.

"However, he isn't out of the woods yet," the doctor continued. "He suffered a mild heart attack, due to several clogged arteries. We need to get him into surgery immediately and clean out those arteries to minimize the risk of another occurrence."

"Angioplasty?" Travis asked.

Dr. Carterson nodded. "It's become a relatively routine procedure, and we don't anticipate any complications. Despite this most recent attack, he's in remarkably good health."

"How soon do you intend to do this?" Francine asked.

"Immediately." Dr. Carterson smiled at Francine. "We only have one small problem. He insists on seeing you before we do anything else."

"Go on," Travis said as he released his hold on her elbow. "I'll wait out here with Gretchen."

She smiled at him gratefully, then followed Dr. Carterson through two sets of swinging doors and into the intensive care unit.

Dwarfed by the huge bed, hooked up to half a dozen machines, Poppy glared at her as she approached. "A man could die from indignity around here," he complained, his voice weak and raspy, but reassuring in its normal gruff tone.

"They've got me wearing a damn gown that's open up the back to show off all my private business," he exclaimed.

"Oh, Poppy, you gave us such a scare," Francine said as she moved to the side of his bed.

"That's why I figured I'd better see you before they wheel me off for some of their witch-doctoring." He shifted positions on the bed, a frown tugging his eyebrows together. "I don't want you thinking you had anything to do with this. That little tiff we had didn't cause me to get sick."

Francine squeezed her eyes closed, allowing his absolution to flow over her. She'd needed to hear him say it, needed to know he didn't blame her for what had happened.

She touched his arm. "Thank you," she said softly.

A nurse walked into the room, a bright smile on her face. "Are we ready for our surgery?" she asked cheerfully.

"We? They cutting you open, too?" Poppy returned irritably.

The nurse smiled and shook her head. "Nobody is cutting you open. You won't even have to be put under general anesthesia." She looked at Francine. "He'll be fine. The doctor will meet you in the waiting room after surgery."

Poppy frowned at Francine. "Go on. Get out of here. I want to get this over with." As she started toward the door, he called after her. "Give Miss Beans a kiss for me."

Francine nodded. When she got back to the waiting

room, Susie was there with Travis and Gretchen. "He's going to be just fine," she told them. "He's as ornery as ever, and he told me to give his Miss Beans a big kiss." She smiled at Gretchen.

"Poppy won't die," Gretchen said to Susie, with the sober certainty of a child. "'Cause heaven don't want him and hell can't handle him." She grinned at Travis. "When you wash out Mommy's mouth, you can wash mine out, too."

Susie laughed and took Gretchen's hand. "How would you like to go to my house and spend the day baking cookies with me?"

Gretchen looked at Francine, who nodded. "I think that's a good idea," Francine said. "It will be a lot more fun baking cookies than sitting here all day."

"Okay. But I'm in my pajamas," Gretchen said, as if it were impossible to bake while clad in night clothes.

"We'll go by your place, and you can change into your baking clothes," Susie said.

Gretchen frowned thoughtfully. "Are overalls baking clothes?" she asked.

"Overalls are the best clothes for anything," Travis answered, his expression so soft, so loving, as he looked at Gretchen.

"Thank you," Francine said to Susie as she walked the two of them out of the waiting room. "It would have been a long day for her if she had to stay here."

Susie smiled. "I'm delighted to have her spend the day with me. In fact, why don't I grab enough clothes so she can spend the night with us? You may want to hang around here late."

Francine hesitated. "Are you sure you wouldn't mind?"

"Mind?" Susie smiled again. "I consider you're doing me a favor."

After Francine gave her daughter a quick round of instructions, Gretchen and Susie disappeared, leaving Francine and Travis alone in the waiting room.

They sat side by side in silence. Francine picked up a magazine, thumbed through it, but couldn't concentrate on any of the articles. All she could think about was the surgery going on somewhere in the hospital, and the man sitting next to her.

She couldn't do anything about Poppy for the moment. He was in the hands of the experienced hospital personnel. However, she could do something to alleviate the sudden tension that had sprung up between herself and Travis.

Closing the magazine on her lap, she turned to look at Travis. "I don't intend to keep her from you," she said softly.

"If you did, I'd fight you every step of the way," he replied.

Francine's back stiffened. "That won't be necessary. We're two reasonable adults. Surely we can come to some sort of a custody agreement where she gets the benefit of both of us loving her."

His eyes were dark and wary. "I thought we were two reasonable adults, but that's before I learned you'd kept her a secret for nearly five years."

Francine sighed. "Travis, I don't want to fight with you."

He seemed to relax slightly, and raked a hand

through his hair. "And I don't want to fight with you."

"It would be nice to know when I leave here that I'd be taking your friendship with me." If she couldn't have his love, friendship would at least be something to hang on to, to cherish when she was so far away.

For a long moment, his gaze held hers, his eyes saying something she couldn't discern, speaking a language she didn't understand. He averted his gaze, as if unable to hold the eye contact any longer. "You'll always have my friendship, Francine," he finally said thickly, as if the words caused him tremendous pain.

"Thank you," she answered, speaking around the lump in her throat. For the first time ever in her long relationship with Travis, she felt the weight of unsaid words, and she wasn't sure if they were her words or his.

It doesn't matter, she told herself, once again picking up the magazine she'd put down moments before. The chapter of her life that had been Travis was over.

She would share their daughter with him, but could no longer envision sharing his life. With her past silence, she'd unknowingly made certain he wouldn't ever want her in his life.

She leaned her head back and closed her eyes, hoping Poppy got back on his feet quickly, so that she could run, escape from the home she'd realized too late she loved.

Francine gave the counter a final swipe, then walked over to the diner door and flipped the Open sign to Closed. It had been two days since Poppy underwent successful surgery. She'd spent all of the first twenty-four hours at the hospital, first waiting for the completion of the surgery, then sitting next to Poppy's bed while he slept.

That morning, Poppy had insisted she work her usual schedule at the diner. He'd told her he didn't want her hovering over him. "If I want to drool in my sleep, I don't want to know you're sitting there watching me," he'd complained.

Francine had kissed him on the forehead and promised to work the afternoon shift at the diner. She'd spoken with Travis, who readily agreed to watch Gretchen while she worked. It was an odd feeling, to drop her daughter off with Travis.

She was going to have to tell Gretchen that Travis was her daddy. Before Travis left the hospital the day Poppy was taken in, she'd asked Travis that he leave it up to her to tell Gretchen. He'd agreed, but she knew that with each moment that passed he grew more anxious for that information to be given to Gretchen.

Tonight, she told herself as she locked up the diner and walked to her car. She'd stop by the hospital for a quick visit with Poppy, then pick up Gretchen, and before the little girl went to bed, Francine would tell her that Travis was her daddy.

It took her only a few minutes to drive to the hospital and find a parking spot in the lot. She parked, then hurried into the building, knowing it was late for a visit, but also knowing the staff would let her sneak in for a quick one.

The nurses at the station nodded to her as she

walked past them and into Poppy's room. He appeared to be asleep. His features were softened with the vulnerability of sleep. She slipped into the chair at his side, not wanting to awaken him, but simply needing a few moments with him.

She sat quietly, studying his face contemplatively. Funny, she wasn't even sure how old he was. She'd always believed him ancient, but she realized now that he couldn't be much older than his mid-sixties.

He wasn't the hateful monster her childish mind had wanted to make him. He'd disciplined hard, but for the most part he'd been fair. He hadn't been a warm, loving man, but she'd spent a lot of time pushing his buttons, testing his limits.

She smiled as she remembered all the times they'd butted heads, hers just as hard and stubborn as his. Perhaps that had been their problem all along.

They were too much alike, too filled with pride and too defensive to put their hearts on their sleeves, where they could easily be wounded.

Poppy stirred and rubbed his eyes, then opened them and looked at her.

"I hope I didn't wake you," she said, steeling herself for a blast of his temperament.

He shook his head and wiped his hands down his face. "You didn't." He sat up, looking slightly disoriented. Once again he rubbed his face, as if attempting to rub away the lingering vestiges of sleep. "I had a dream."

"A good one, I hope."

"Good and bad." He stared at Francine, his gaze seeming to pierce through her skin and into her soul. "I dreamed of your mama."

"Oh." Francine wasn't sure what to say, exactly what to expect.

He frowned. "Pull your chair up here closer. We need to talk, Frannie girl."

Francine moved her chair closer, wondering where this was leading, fearing unfamiliar territory about to be explored.

"In my dream, your mama was mad at me. Said I was letting her down by not telling you some things you need to hear." Poppy shook his head, a soft smile transforming his face into something beautiful that Francine had never seen before. "Your mama always did have a temper."

"This is the first time you've ever talked about her," Francine observed.

Poppy stared up at the ceiling. "I never could before. It hurt too much." He looked back at Francine, his faded blue eyes sparkling with unshed tears. "She was my only child, the light in my heart."

For the first time, Francine realized the depths of his loss. When she arrived at his house, an angry, grieving ten-year-old, he'd just discovered his only child was gone. "Oh, Poppy, I never realized..." She reached out and took his hand in hers.

For a moment, his remained unmoving. Then he looked down at their hands, and as a tear fell down his cheek, he curled his fingers around hers. "I was so buried in my own hurt, I didn't know how to help you with yours," he said.

Once again he gazed at her, taking in her features bit by bit. "And there you were," he continued, "a little miniature of my baby, and I'd never been so scared in my whole life."

She looked at him in surprise. "Scared? Why?"

He smiled and his hand tightened around hers. "What did I know about raising a kid? When your mama was little, Della was there to do the raising. But it was just you and me, and you were the most needy kid I'd ever seen."

"I just wanted you to love me," Francine said, her voice husky with suppressed emotion.

"I was afraid if I was too soft, you'd run wild and get into trouble and them social workers would think I was unfit to raise you. I was just plain too scared to show you any sort of love. I was too overwhelmed with the responsibility of being your only parent."

Francine felt as if the past as she knew it were suddenly exploding apart. She had never viewed the situation from Poppy's perspective, had possessed only the tunnel vision and self-centeredness that came with youth.

He smiled at her. "Of course, it's easy with Miss Beans. I can love her and not feel responsible for her. She's your child to raise, I just get to be Poppy with her."

"And she makes it easy to love her, where I fought you every step of the way," Francine said.

"We fought each other. But maybe it's not too late to change that?" He seemed to hold his breath as he waited for her reply.

She released her hold on his hand and leaned over and hugged him. His arms wrapped around her back, patting her, as if comforting the needy child she had been. A healing warmth flowed through her, reaching into the deepest, darkest corners of her soul, filling them with light and love.

"I love you, Frannie girl," he whispered softly. "I've always loved you."

"And I love you, Poppy."

"Now let go of me before you strangle me to death," he said gruffly.

Laughing, she swiped her tears and sat back down. She knew instinctively that they would never talk of such things again. Once they left this room, Poppy would still be cantankerous and Francine would still get irritated, but beneath it all would be the strong pillar of love they'd erected at this moment.

"They're letting me out of here tomorrow," he said.

"What time? I'll be here to pick you up."

He shook his head. "I already made arrangements for Travis to come get me. That way you don't have to drag Miss Beans down here."

"You know we wouldn't mind," Francine protested.

He nodded. "I know, but it's already done. Travis will come to get me."

Francine shrugged and stood. "Whatever. It will just be nice to have you home again."

"Frannie...about you leaving Cooperville." He frowned and puckered his lips thoughtfully. "I suppose I should apologize for giving you a hard time. I want you to be happy, and if that means living in New York City, then I want you to go. But I would like it if you'd write more often, and maybe call once in a while, let me talk to Miss Beans."

She leaned down and kissed him on the forehead. "I think we can handle that. But don't worry, we aren't going anywhere until I'm sure you're back on your feet.''

"The doc says I'm fit as a fiddle. All I need is to get home and eat something besides the gruel they've been feeding me here.''

Francine smiled. "I'll make sure we have a special meal just for your homecoming tomorrow,'' she promised.

"Don't go to no trouble.'' He smiled slyly. "Although pot roast and homemade biscuits sure would hit the spot.''

"You've got it.'' She started for the door. "I'll see you tomorrow.''

He nodded. "Frannie, I do love you.''

Her heart expanded, filled her chest with soothing warmth. "I love you, too, Poppy.''

The warmth continued to suffuse her as she drove to Travis's to pick up Gretchen. This time, when she left for New York, she'd know she had Poppy's love with her. She'd write him often and she knew he'd write her back, each letter containing pieces of the foundation of caring they'd discovered within each other.

If things had been different with Travis, she would have considered staying here. But with her love for him so deep, she knew staying would prove too difficult.

Still, she was committed to making sure that Gretchen got to spend plenty of time with both Travis and Poppy. Gretchen was a very lucky little girl—her life was filled with people who loved her.

She pulled up in front of Travis's house and left the car running as she walked up to the front porch.

He met her at the door. "Come on in. She's in the living room," he said as he opened the door.

"Thanks for watching her while I worked. I appreciate it," she said as she stepped into the house.

He shrugged, his gaze dark and distant. "It's what daddies do." He started into the living room, but hesitated when Francine touched his arm.

"I'm going to tell her tonight."

His eyes lightened with anticipation. "Should I be there when you tell her?"

Francine shook her head. "No, I need to do this alone." Together they walked into the living room, where Gretchen was stretched out on the floor, coloring a picture.

"Hi, Mommy," she said. "I drew a picture of the kittens. I'm coloring it, and Uncle Travis says he'll hang it on his refrigerator door."

"I'm sure it will look very nice on his refrigerator," Francine answered. She didn't want to look at Travis. Seeing him brought an unbearable pain to her heart.

"I'm almost done," Gretchen said as she focused back on her work. She moved the crayon across the page, then sat up. "There," she said, to indicate that her masterpiece was finished.

She got up and handed the colored drawing to Travis. "This is the finest picture I believe I've ever seen," Travis said, his words making Gretchen beam.

"Tell Travis thank-you," Francine instructed. "It's getting late, and we need to get home."

"Thank you, Uncle Travis. I had a fun day." She reached up to give him a hug.

"I'm glad," he replied. "And I promise we'll have

lots of fun days together in the future.'' As he hugged Gretchen, Francine shoved away the ache in her heart.

There's nothing worse than the ache of unrequited love, she thought a moment later, as she and Gretchen drove toward Poppy's house. She was filled with love for Travis, but that love had nowhere to go, nothing to do.

How long did it take for love to eventually die? Five years in a distant city hadn't managed to kill her love for him. When would she finally be able to think of him, see him, and not want him, not ache deep inside from that want?

At least by going to New York she would place some distance between them. She'd no longer see him every day, no longer be subjected to the sound of his deep, pleasant laughter drifting on an evening breeze. His scent wouldn't linger in the air after him, taunting her with memories.

Perhaps in New York City she could meet somebody new for herself, someone who could banish the memories of the handsome farmer who'd shared a night of passion with her beneath a full summer moon.

However, before she could try to forget Travis, before she attempted to diminish him in her own life, she had to give him his proper place in her daughter's life.

Francine waited until Gretchen was in bed, her little face shining from a vigorous washing. Sitting on the edge of the cot, Francine smoothed a strand of Gretchen's shiny hair away from her face, wondering where to begin.

"We need to have a little talk," she began.

Gretchen frowned. "Am I in trouble?"

"Have you done something to make you think you might be in trouble?" Francine returned.

"I don't think so, but sometimes you get mad over stuff that I don't think you should be mad about."

Francine smiled. "Well, I'm not mad about anything, and what I want to talk to you about should make you very happy."

Gretchen sat up, her features lit with curiosity. "What? Tell me, Mommy."

"You know most little girls have a mommy and a daddy."

Gretchen nodded. "Mary Elizabeth at day care has had three daddies. Her real one and two step ones."

"Well, you don't have any step ones, but you have a real one."

"I do?" Gretchen's eyes opened wide.

Francine drew a deep breath. "Travis is your real daddy."

"He is?" Gretchen clapped her hands together in childish glee. "Oh, I'm so happy. I love Uncle Travis." She stopped and frowned at Francine thoughtfully. "But I thought real mommies and daddies were married. How come you're not married to Uncle Travis?"

"Sometimes real mommies and daddies are married and sometimes they're not," Francine answered, ignoring the ache of her heart. Sometimes things didn't work out. Sometimes they just didn't love each other enough.

"Can I call him Daddy?"

Francine's heart expanded. "Yes, I think he'd like

that very much. And when we get back to New York you can come in the summers to visit him.''

''I don't want to go back to New York.'' Gretchen's lower lip trembled ominously. ''I like it here with Poppy and Uncle...Daddy. I want to stay here forever and ever.''

''Gretchen, you knew all along we just came back here to visit, but our home is in New York,'' Francine said patiently.

''But I don't want my home to be in New York,'' she replied, tears filling her eyes and spilling onto her cheeks. ''I want my home to be here. I like it here best of all. Beauty likes it better here, too.''

Gretchen had never been a child who cried easily, and her silent sobs ripped through Francine. She rubbed her eyes with her fists as she continued to cry. Francine pulled the child into her arms and patted her back, wishing for a way to turn her tears into smiles.

Gretchen's sobs slowed to an occasional hiccup, and she finally looked at Francine once again. ''Mommy, Poppy needs us here. If I'm not here, who is going to feed the bunnies? Who's going to make Poppy laugh? If I'm not here, he'll forget how to smile.''

She sat up, slipping out of Francine's embrace. ''Why can't we just stay here? I have a mommy, a daddy and a Poppy here. In stinky old New York I don't have anything.''

Francine sighed. ''I think maybe we've talked enough about it tonight. It's time for you to go to sleep.'' She kissed Gretchen's forehead, where a frown remained.

''I'll probably never go to sleep now,'' Gretchen

protested, "and if I do I'll probably have bad dreams," she added with a touch of self-pity. She closed her eyes and, despite her words to the contrary, within moments she was sound asleep.

Francine undressed, then slipped into her nightgown. Instead of going to sleep, she sat on the end of her bed and stared thoughtfully at her daughter, sleeping on the nearby cot.

She wanted Gretchen to grow up happy, in the best environment, with people she loved surrounding her. As Gretchen had reminded her, here in Cooperville the little girl had a Poppy and a daddy. In New York City, she only had a mother who had to work to survive.

Granted, remaining in Cooperville would be the best possible thing for Gretchen—but it would be the most painful thing for Francine.

She'd have to see Travis often, deal with him, because of their mutual love for their child. And every time she saw him, every time she heard his voice, she'd ache inside, knowing he'd never love her as she did him.

She had to weigh her pain against Gretchen's happiness, and in that particular battle, there was no contest. Gretchen would always come first, and her best chance for a happy, healthy childhood was here in Cooperville.

The worst part would be swallowing her pride, telling everyone she'd changed her mind. She slid beneath the sheets on her bed and tried to relax. Maybe she just wouldn't tell anyone she'd changed her mind. She'd simply never leave.

Eventually it will stop hurting, she told herself.

Eventually she'd forget Travis and the magic that had once existed between them.

Maybe she'd go out with Barry. The newspaperman had been attractive, and seemed nice enough. She closed her eyes and tried to conjure up some excitement at the idea, but dread was all she felt.

Even if she never dated another man, she could lead a full life here, working in the diner, taking care of Poppy and Gretchen. She could even do some volunteer work in the community. It could be a good life.

She closed her eyes and thought about the dreams of stardom she'd once entertained. The childhood dreams of a lonely, unloved little girl. Those goals seemed silly now, empty. She didn't mourn the death of that particular dream. What she mourned was that she'd never be a part of those wonderful dreams Travis had spun.

"Who needs dreams?" she whispered softly, then squeezed her eyes tightly closed against the tears that threatened to fall.

Chapter Eleven

"You comfortable enough?" Travis asked Poppy as he pulled the car out of the hospital parking lot.

"Fine. I'd be happy to ride a camel if it meant getting out of that place. I never tasted such bad food in my life, and all them nurses talked to me like I was either senile or deaf." Poppy snorted.

Travis bit back a smile. He'd heard the nurses had taken up a collection, intending to bribe the doctor into releasing Poppy, who was apparently not the best patient in the world.

"Actually, I feel better than I have in months," Poppy continued. "Guess the old ticker needed a little more maintenance than I realized." He thumped his chest with two fingers. "But since they did that balloon trick, I feel ten years younger."

"I'm glad, Poppy. You scared the hell out of all of us." Travis tightened his grip on the steering wheel as he remembered walking into Poppy's kitchen and finding the old man on the floor.

He hadn't realized the depth of his feelings for Poppy until that moment. He hadn't realized how much Poppy had filled a void inside him until he contemplated life without the old man.

Poppy laughed. "I have to admit, I scared the hell out of myself." He sobered and looked at Travis. "I'm not ready to die yet. I got things to do, amends to make."

Travis shot him a sideways glance. "Amends?"

Poppy nodded and leaned back against the seat, his brow wrinkled in thought. "Sometimes a man thinks he's doing the right things, taking care of business and responsibilities, and he forgets what's important and what's not."

Again Travis looked at him, unsure what he was talking about. "I'm not sure I understand," he said.

Poppy sighed. "No, I don't suppose you do. I doubt you made the same kind of mistakes I made."

Travis still didn't understand what he was talking about. As Poppy turned his gaze out the window, Travis realized he didn't seem particularly inclined to explain.

For a few minutes, they rode in silence. As always, when there was a moment of quiet, Travis's thoughts turned to Francine. And as always, thoughts of her brought with them a sadness mingled with anger.

The fact that she had kept Gretchen a secret for so long boggled his mind. The fact that she intended to leave Cooperville once again tore him up inside. Not only because she'd be taking his daughter with her, but also because she'd be taking his heart.

"You going to let her leave you again?"

Travis shot a startled look at Poppy, wondering if

the old man had the power to read his mind. "I can't stop her."

"Yes, you can," Poppy said challengingly. "I figure you're about the only one who can stop her."

"And how do you suggest I do that?" he asked.

"You love her, don't you?"

Travis didn't answer for a long moment. Despite the fact that he was still angry with Francine, in spite of his feeling of betrayal, beneath it all was still the deep, abiding love he'd always felt for her. "What difference does it make? She doesn't want me. I'm not sure Frannie even knows what love is," he added bitterly.

Poppy nodded. "You might be right about that. Lord knows I didn't show her much when she was growing up. I figure it's going to take a very special kind of man to fill the holes I left in our girl." He gazed slyly at Travis. "I thought you might be that man."

"You love her, too. Surely you could make her stay," Travis countered.

Poppy sighed, a deep expression of regret. "No, she needed my love when she was a little girl, and I let her down. But she's a woman now, and it isn't my love she needs to give her a reason to stay."

A reason to stay. Travis desperately wished he could give her that. But he'd never be enough for her. His dreams, his life, were simple. It would never be enough for her. "I loved her five years ago, and she had no trouble walking away," Travis reminded Poppy.

"Did you tell her you loved her then? Did you ask her to stay?"

"No. I didn't want to be the reason she stayed. I didn't want her to someday resent me for stealing her dreams from her." Travis slowed the truck as they approached Poppy's driveway.

"Dreams." Poppy spit out the word, as if it left a disgusting taste in his mouth. "I think the two of you did far too much dreaming and not enough loving. Dreams are fine until they get in between two people who love each other."

"If Francine really loved me, she'd have told me about Gretchen years ago," Travis said angrily as he pulled to a stop before the house.

"If she didn't love you, she wouldn't have told you at all." Poppy got out of the truck, then leaned back in the window. "Frannie promised me a big roast for dinner. Want to come in and eat?"

"No, thanks," Travis answered absently. He needed to think. Poppy's words had confused him, caused the core of anger he'd felt for the past couple of days to ebb.

"Thanks for the ride home," Poppy said. "You're the only one who can do it, Travis. Give her a reason to stay." Without waiting for his reply, Poppy turned and walked toward the house.

Travis peeled out of the driveway, irritated by the entire conversation, tantalized by Poppy's view that somehow he could change Francine's mind.

As if anyone could change Frannie's mind. She was the most stubborn, willful woman Travis had ever known. Surely she knew he loved her desperately. Surely she couldn't doubt that he'd always dreamed they'd have a life together.

Dreams. Was Poppy right? Had they spent too

much time fantasizing about futures that had little to do with reality? She'd returned to Cooperville not the star she'd pretended, but out of money and out of work—a far cry from her childhood dreams.

Her dream for celebrity and his for family had at the root of them one basic theme. The need to be loved. They had both wanted that desperately. He knew she'd needed to feel special, to feel loved, because her life with Poppy had been so lacking in that emotion. As for him, he'd simply wanted to be loved by her.

Had they held their real dream in their hands all along, and let it fly from their fingertips like tiny bits of grain blowing in the wind?

In asking Francine to stay, he'd be putting his pride squarely on the line. He would be giving her another chance to either accept his love or walk away from him.

He wasn't sure he wanted to risk it. He wasn't sure he could handle it if, for the second time in their life, she made the conscious choice to walk away from his love. Easier not to put his heart on the line than to put it in a position to be kicked.

At least I'll have Gretchen, he thought. Even though it would probably only be for a couple weeks each summer and various holidays, her visits would be joyous occasions to eagerly anticipate.

Surely he had enough to fill his life without Francine. He'd have his time with Gretchen, Susie would be having a baby, and Margaret would eventually get married and have children. Yes, his life would be quite full without Francine.

He wasn't the special man Poppy had spoken

about. He wasn't the man to teach Francine about love. Travis was just a simple man who would never be enough for a woman like Francine.

"More roast?" Francine asked Poppy. It was just the two of them at the table. Gretchen had finished eating and begged to be excused, as there was a family of new bunnies in the hutch that just had to be watched.

"I couldn't eat another bite of anything," he said as he patted his stomach. "That was the finest roast I've tasted since your grandma used to make it every Sunday."

Francine glowed beneath the compliment. "I used Grandma's recipe. I found a notebook of all her recipes upstairs in the spare room."

Poppy eyed her in surprise. "What were you doing in there?"

"I was wondering if you would mind if I sort of fixed up that room for Gretchen. We may be here a while longer, and I think it would be better if we both had our own space."

"Sure. Do whatever you want up there. That room's always been sort of a catchall. Anything you don't want can be stored in the smokehouse."

Francine felt the unspoken questions Poppy had, knew he was wondering why she was planning to redecorate a room if her plan was to leave.

She didn't explain to him that she'd changed her mind about leaving, that Gretchen's happiness was far more important than her unhappiness at losing Travis's love. She simply felt too vulnerable to talk about the loss of all her dreams, the loss of love.

Of course, she'd discovered something special with Poppy, a love previously unexplored, and that would certainly help her heal. But there would always be scars on her heart from loving Travis, scars that nothing and nobody could heal.

"I think I'll take a little walk down to the hutch and help Miss Beans with the rabbits," Poppy said as he shoved away from the table. He started toward the back door, but the jangle of the phone made him stop in his tracks. "I'll get it," he said. He reached for the receiver of the wall phone as Francine began to clear the dishes from the table.

"Hi, Betty Jean." Poppy listened for a moment, then looked at Francine. "Of course she can. No, it's not a problem. You just take care of yourself, and I'll send Francine right over."

"Over where?" Francine asked as soon as he'd hung up.

"To the diner. Betty Jean was supposed to work from noon until close, but about an hour ago she got feeling poorly. She's running a fever and is feeling sick to her stomach." Poppy cast Francine a small smile. "I got a feeling a sick waitress might not be good for business."

Francine ignored his humor. "How can I go to work now? I don't want to leave you and Gretchen. You just got out of the hospital."

"The way I understand it, when you get out of the hospital, it means you're well. Miss Beans and I will be fine, and I'll finish clearing the table. You go on and relieve Betty Jean. Go on," he repeated when Francine didn't move.

"Poppy…"

"Please, Frannie. We'll be fine, and if I feel the least bit tired, I'll call Travis to help me out."

Francine hesitated another moment, then wiped her hands on a towel and picked up her car keys from the counter. She had the feeling the idea of the diner without adequate help on a Saturday night would be far more stressful for him than an evening at home with Gretchen. "Okay, but only if you promise me you won't try to overdo things while I'm gone."

"I promise," Poppy answered.

By the time Francine got to the diner, the Saturday dinner rush was on. The one waitress, a high school student working part-time, nearly sobbed in relief when Francine walked through the door.

For the next three hours, Francine had no time for thoughts or worries. She served, cleaned tables, chatted with customers and took money without taking a moment to breathe.

By eight, the crowd had thinned out enough that she could pour herself a cup of coffee and sink down on a stool to catch her breath.

She knew there wouldn't be much time for a break. Usually on Saturdays, about the time the older dinner group stopped, the teenage trade began and kept up a steady pace until closing.

It was nearly nine when a truck pulled up in the parking space directly outside the diner front door. She recognized Travis's truck, and for a moment fear shot through her. Had something happened to Poppy? Was Gretchen all right?

When he didn't come inside, she walked out to where he remained seated in his truck. "Is Poppy all right?" she asked.

He nodded, a muscle working overtime in his jaw. "He and Gretchen are fine. I stopped by there before coming here."

"Oh." She eyed him curiously. "Are you going to come in?"

"I haven't decided yet." Again the muscle in his jaw twitched rhythmically.

A carload of teens pulled up nearby. They spilled out of the car and headed inside. "I've got to get back to work," Francine said, wondering exactly what he was doing out here. Realizing no answer was forthcoming, she turned and went back into the diner.

For the next two hours, the place hopped with the young crowd of Cooperville. However, no matter how busy it got, Francine couldn't keep her mind on work. She found herself constantly looking out the window, where Travis remained in his truck.

Even through the thick glass, she could feel his dark, heated gaze on her. His concentration seemed to be solely on her.

What was he doing out there? Why was he just sitting there watching her? It was more than a little disconcerting. She wished he'd go away. She wished he'd come inside. More than anything, she wished he loved her.

Travis watched her as she worked. Despite the anger he wanted to feel for her, he found himself wishing he could tangle his fingers in her long, dark hair, taste the sweetness of her lips, hold her in his arms and feel their hearts beating together.

Poppy's words had confused him. Francine's actions since she came back home had perplexed him, too. He remembered that moment in the cornfield, when in the middle of playing hide-and-seek they had kissed. Their passion had ignited instantaneously. And then, in that same field, when she'd flashed him their signal to meet.

Was it possible for her to feel such desire for him and not love him? Despite the fact that he'd raised his two sisters, he didn't know much about the ways and thoughts of women. And Frannie had always been as enigmatic as they came. So, what was in her heart?

She hadn't come running back to Cooperville because she desperately missed him. She'd come back because she was broke.

He didn't want the broken pieces left from her shattered dreams. He didn't want to be the consolation prize she won for failing to achieve what she'd always dreamed of.

And yet, though it had been late in coming, she'd given him his dream, the greatest gift a woman could give a man...a child.

He leaned his head back against the seat and thought of Gretchen. When he stopped by Poppy's earlier, the little girl had greeted him with a hug and a kiss.

"Mommy said that you're my real daddy," she'd said. "I'm so glad, 'cause I love you, Uncle... Daddy."

Those words had caused a lump of emotion to fill his throat, and he'd realized that no matter what happened between him and Frannie, his daughter was his forever.

Still, Poppy's words haunted him, confused him

and irritated him. The old man had hinted that a future with Frannie was his, if he'd only reach out and take it.

Could he make her happy? Could he give her a new dream, his dream? Certainly he knew he would never love another woman as he loved Frannie. She was in his heart, etched in his soul. Was he in hers?

He unbuckled his seat belt and opened the door. It was time to find out. The cowbell jangled, announcing his arrival, and Frannie looked up from her order pad, surprise and a touch of wariness darkening her eyes.

"We need to talk," he said without preamble as he reached her. "Come outside with me."

"This isn't exactly a good time," she said. One of the teenagers at the table snickered, but the sly laughter died as Travis froze the boy with a glare.

"I'll wait." He walked over to the counter and slid onto a stool.

He could tell his presence made her nervous. She dropped the order pad, picked it up and finished writing the order. Her fingers trembled slightly.

She obviously had no idea why he was here. She probably believed he wanted to fight about custody arrangements for Gretchen.

He didn't want to fight. And he wasn't about to play spiteful games where Gretchen was concerned. He wanted to know if they had a future together. He needed to know if she intended to leave him yet again. A blossom of anger filled his chest at that thought.

Suddenly he couldn't wait. He stood and advanced on her. "We have to talk now."

"Travis, I'm working here," she protested.

"Karen, take over for Frannie," he said to the teenage waitress. He took Frannie's hand and with single-minded determination tugged her outside.

"Travis, you're making a scene," she hissed as they left the cool interior of the diner and stepped out into the heat of the night. "Have you lost your mind?" she snapped. She jerked her wrist out of his grip and faced him angrily.

"Yes, I have lost my mind. I've become completely irrational, utterly mad, and it's all your fault." He glared at her, and for a moment he wondered if he had gone around the bend. He'd been half-crazy since the moment she returned, alternating between loving her and wanting to hate her.

"What are you talking about?" she asked.

"I want to know when you intend to leave town."

She paused thoughtfully before answering him. "What difference does it make?" she countered. "I told you I'd make certain you get plenty of time with Gretchen."

"I'm not talking about Gretchen. I'm talking about you and me."

She frowned, a small wrinkle appearing across her forehead. "What about you and me? There is no you and me."

"That's because you ran out on me five years ago." The words exploded out of him, and he realized that was why thoughts of her always brought a touch of anger. Because he'd needed her. She'd been his sanity, and she'd left him. While he was so overwhelmed with his family responsibilities, Frannie had been the sunshine in his life.

"I'm not going to rehash all of this again," she

said angrily. "We've already done that, and it only makes us say things we regret." She whirled around to leave, but he caught her by the shoulders and forced her to face him again.

"I don't intend to say anything I regret." He held on to her shoulders, not wanting her to escape before he had his say. "That night you left, I watched you." His voice thickened as he remembered the sickness in his stomach as he'd watched her disappear from his view, from his life. "I hid in the corn and hoped, prayed, you'd stop, that you'd realize that you wanted me more than you wanted your dreams. That somehow your dream would be me."

Her features, splashed with a pink glow from the blinking neon light nearby, displayed surprise. "Then why didn't you stop me? You didn't love me enough to stop me from leaving."

He raked a hand through his hair and dropped his hands to his sides. "Oh, Frannie, I didn't stop you from going because I loved you too much, not because I didn't love you enough." He shoved his hands in his pockets. "How could I stop you? I couldn't be the one to prevent you from chasing after your dreams. I didn't want to force you to stay, only to have you later resent me."

Francine wrapped her arms around her shoulders, studying his face reflectively. "I wanted you to stop me. I hoped you would. All I wanted was for you to tell me to stay, tell me that you loved me."

"I thought my love would be a burden to you."

She smiled softly. "And I thought Gretchen would be a burden to you. I guess we worked at cross-purposes, trying to protect each other and hurting each other in the process.''

"I never wanted to hurt you,'' he said. Her words caused a final healing inside him. She had loved him, had wanted to remain. But that had been five years ago. What did she want now?

"Maybe I would have grown to resent you, had I not gone to New York.'' Again her features grew reflective. "Maybe I needed the past five years to grow up, to realize exactly what was important to me.''

"And what is important to you?'' Travis felt as if his breath were lodged in his throat.

"This town. Poppy.'' She drew in an unsteady breath. "We aren't leaving, Travis. We're staying here.'' To his surprise, her eyes filled with tears. "Gretchen wants to stay here where she has a daddy and a Poppy.''

"And what do you want?''

Her eyes shimmered, and tears spilled down her cheeks. "What do I want? I want to stop loving you, so it won't hurt so much to see you. I wish that I could forget that you loved me once, and I blew it.''

Travis's heart leaped at her words. Was it possible that cantankerous old man had been right? That all Frannie needed was to know he loved her?

He pulled his hands from his pockets and placed them on either side of her face, caressing the smooth skin of her cheeks with his thumbs. "Now why in the hell would you want to stop loving me, when I love you so desperately?''

Her eyes widened. "You what?''

"I love you, Frannie. Yesterday...today... always.''

A sob choked from her, and she leaned into him and closed her eyes. "Say it again," she whispered.

"I love you. I've always loved you. I will always love you." He wrapped his arms around her, enfolding her close to his chest. Her heart beat rapidly against his. He could hear the frantic pounding, and knew it was the sound of love.

She tilted her head back to look at him, her eyes shining, not with tears, but with love. "Oh, Travis, sometimes I think I was born loving you. I know I'll die loving you."

He bent his head and captured her lips with his. The kiss was fiery, containing the passion, the desire, the love, of a lifetime. "Marry me," he whispered when he broke the kiss. "Marry me, and let's build dreams together."

"If I marry you, I'll have my dream," she answered breathlessly.

He smiled down at her. "Can I take that as a yes?"

"Yes, oh, yes."

Again Travis covered her mouth with his, wanting to lose himself in her lips, knowing he would spend the rest of his life loving her.

As his lips plied hers, he became aware of the sound of cheering. He broke the kiss and looked at the diner window, where a bevy of teenagers were looking out, hooting and hollering as if cheering on their favorite sports hero.

A blush stained Francine's cheeks as she started to step back from him. "We'll be the talk of the town by morning."

He grinned. "Then let's really give them something to talk about,'' he replied, and pulled her back into his arms.

''For a simple man, you have a way of making me feel very special,'' she said with a sigh as he nuzzled the sweet flesh of her neck.

''You are special, Frannie. You're my girl...now and for always.'' He kissed her again, the sounds of the teenagers fading from his mind as he gave himself completely to the simple joy of loving Frannie.

Epilogue

Francine sat in front of her bedroom window, staring out on the moonlit landscape. She should be asleep. It would soon be midnight, and tomorrow would be a full day.

She wrapped her arms around herself and leaned her forehead against the cold glass of the window. It was hard to believe two months had passed since the night Travis proposed to her in front of the diner. Two months of more laughter and happiness than she'd ever dreamed possible.

A flash of light shone from Travis's window, a quick flash followed by another one. She smiled and realized why she hadn't been sleepy. She'd known, with the intuitiveness that had always marked their relationship, that Travis would signal to meet her tonight.

She grabbed a jacket from her closet, knowing the chill of a late-October night. Shrugging it on, she walked into the next room, where Gretchen was in bed.

Gretchen slept on her side, one arm hugging the stuffed dinosaur her daddy had won for her at the carnival. Content that Gretchen slept soundly, Francine went back into her own room and silently slipped out the window.

The cold night air whipped around her as she ran toward Travis, who stood in the middle of the field. Joy filled her as he opened his arms to her.

Her body met his and rejoiced in the familiar contours of their embrace. For a long moment they merely stood, hugging each other, with no need for words.

"I wasn't sure you'd see my signal," he said as he reluctantly released her.

She smiled. "I was expecting it."

"Ah, you know me too well." He sat on the ground and tugged her hand so that she would sit next to him as they had done a hundred—a thousand— nights in the past.

"You're lucky I came. It's unlucky for a groom to see his bride on their wedding day."

Travis held his hand up to the moonlight and looked at his watch. "We still have fifteen minutes before it's officially our wedding day."

She leaned against him. "Nervous?" she asked.

He placed an arm around her and pulled her close to his side. "Not a bit. What about you?"

She snuggled closer. "Not at all. I feel like marrying you is the most right thing I've ever done in my life." She looked up at the moon, wondering how it could be that wishes she'd never known she possessed were coming true. "Who'd have thought Poppy would insist we have a traditional wedding?"

Travis laughed, the pleasant sound sending a shiver of delight up Francine's spine. "I think Poppy is a closet romantic. I swear I saw tears in his eyes when we were picking out the flowers."

Francine smiled. Yes, Poppy was a continual surprise. The simple family ceremony Travis and Francine had imagined had grown as Poppy took over the arrangements.

"Speaking of flowers, Gretchen has decided I shouldn't carry any."

"Why?" Travis asked in surprise.

"She says it's so close to Halloween, it would be better if I carried a jack-o'-lantern."

"I don't care if you carry a black cat and wear a witch's cape, as long as you are at the church and say, 'I do.'" He kissed her—a deep kiss that made her mind spin and her heartbeat quicken.

"I love you, Frannie," he said when he broke the kiss. "I promise I'll spend the rest of my life trying to make you happy. I'll make sure you'll never regret staying here."

"Shhh." She placed a finger against his lips. "I only have one regret, and it's that five years ago I was too proud, too stubborn, to tell you what I really needed." She placed her hands on either side of his face, looking at the masculine features she loved with all her heart, all her soul. "I love you, Travis, and you're all I need to make my dreams come true."

Once again his lips covered hers, in a kiss that tasted of both passion and tenderness, past and future. In some place deep in the back of her mind, Francine said a silent goodbye to her childhood dreams...and welcomed the new ones she'd found with this simple man she loved.

* * * * *

ELIZABETH AUGUST

Continues the twelve-book series—36 HOURS—in November 1997 with Book Five

CINDERELLA STORY

Life was hardly a fairy tale for Nina Lindstrom. Out of work and with an ailing child, the struggling single mom was running low on hope. Then Alex Bennett solved her problems with one convenient proposal: marriage. And though he had made no promises beyond financial security, Nina couldn't help but feel that with a little love, happily-ever-afters really could come true!

For Alex and Nina and *all* the residents of Grand Springs, Colorado, the storm-induced blackout was just the beginning of 36 Hours that changed *everything!* You won't want to miss a single book.

Take 4 bestselling love stories FREE

Plus get a FREE surprise gift!

He's able to change a diaper in three seconds flat.
And melt an unsuspecting heart even quicker.
But changing his mind about marriage might take some doing!
He's more than a man...
He's a FABULOUS FATHER!

***

September 1997:
WANTED: ONE SON by Laurie Paige (#1246)
Deputy sheriff Nick Dorelli's heart ached for fatherless Doogie Clay—the boy who should have been *his* son—and the woman who should have been *his* wife. Could they all be blessed with a second chance?

November 1997:
WIFE WITHOUT A PAST by Elizabeth Harbison (#1258)
Drew Bennett had raised his child alone. But then the single dad discovered his former bride Laura was *alive*—but didn't remember their wedded estate! Could he make this wife without a past learn to love again?

January 1998:
THE BILLIONAIRE'S BABY CHASE by Valerie Parv (#1270)
Zoe loved little Genie as her own, so when the little girl's handsome billionaire father appeared out of the blue to claim her, Zoe had only one choice—to marry James Langford in a marriage of convenience.

***

Celebrate fatherhood—and love!—every month.
FABULOUS FATHERS...only in 🕊 *Silhouette* ROMANCE™

As seen on TV!
Free Gift Offer

With a Free Gift proof-of-purchase from any Silhouette® book,
you can receive a beautiful cubic zirconia pendant.

This gorgeous marquise-shaped stone is a genuine cubic
zirconia—accented by an 18" gold tone necklace.
(Approximate retail value $19.95)

Send for yours today…
compliments of ▼ *Silhouette*®
™

To receive your free gift, a cubic zirconia pendant, send us one original proof-of-
purchase, photocopies not accepted, from the back of any Silhouette Romance™,
Silhouette Desire®, Silhouette Special Edition®, Silhouette Intimate Moments®
or Silhouette Yours Truly™ title available at your favorite retail outlet, together with
the Free Gift Certificate, plus a check or money order for $1.65 U.S./$2.15 CAN. (do
not send cash) to cover postage and handling, payable to Silhouette Free Gift Offer.
We will send you the specified gift. Allow 6 to 8 weeks for delivery. Offer good until
December 31, 1997, or while quantities last. Offer valid in the U.S. and Canada only.

Free Gift Certificate

Name: _____

Address: _____

City: _____ State/Province: _____ Zip/Postal Code: _____

Mail this certificate, one proof-of-purchase and a check or money order for postage
and handling to: SILHOUETTE FREE GIFT OFFER 1997. In the U.S.: 3010 Walden
Avenue, P.O. Box 9077, Buffalo NY 14269-9077. In Canada: P.O. Box 613, Fort Erie,
Ontario L2Z 5X3.

FREE GIFT OFFER   084-KFD
ONE PROOF-OF-PURCHASE
To collect your fabulous FREE GIFT, a cubic zirconia pendant, you must include this
original proof-of-purchase for each gift with the properly completed Free Gift Certificate.

084-KFDR

SILHOUETTE WOMEN KNOW ROMANCE WHEN THEY SEE IT.

And they'll see it on **ROMANCE CLASSICS**, the new 24-hour TV channel devoted to romantic movies and original programs like the special **Romantically Speaking—Harlequin™ Goes Prime Time.**

Romantically Speaking—Harlequin™ Goes Prime Time introduces you to many of your favorite romance authors in a program developed exclusively for Harlequin® and Silhouette® readers.

Watch for **Romantically Speaking—Harlequin™ Goes Prime Time** beginning in the summer of 1997.

If you're not receiving ROMANCE CLASSICS, call your local cable operator or satellite provider and ask for it today!

ROMANCE CLASSICS

Escape to the network of your dreams.

See Ingrid Bergman and Gregory Peck in *Spellbound* on Romance Classics.

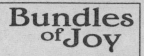

Bundles of JOY

Babies have a way of bringing out the love in everyone's hearts! And Silhouette Romance is delighted to present you with three wonderful new love stories.

October:
DADDY WOKE UP MARRIED by Julianna Morris (SR#1252)
Emily married handsome Nick Carleton temporarily to give her unborn child a name. Then a tumble off the roof left this amnesiac daddy-to-be thinking lovely Emily was his *real* wife, and was she enjoying it! But what would happen when Nick regained his memory?

December:
THE BABY CAME C.O.D. by Marie Ferrarella (SR#1264)
(Two Halves of a Whole)
Tycoon Evan Quartermain found a *baby* in his office—with a note saying the adorable little girl was his! Luckily next-door neighbor and pretty single mom Claire was glad to help out, and soon Evan was forgoing corporate takeovers in favor of baby rattles and long, sultry nights with the beautiful Claire!

February:
Silhouette Romance is pleased to present ON BABY PATROL by Sharon DeVita, (SR#1276), which is also the first of her new *Lullabies and Love* series. A legendary cradle brings the three rugged Sullivan brothers unexpected love, fatherhood and family.

Don't miss these adorable Bundles of Joy, only from

Silhouette ROMANCE™

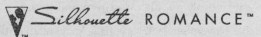

Daniel MacGregor is at it again…

New York Times bestselling author

NORA ROBERTS

introduces us to a new generation of MacGregors
as the lovable patriarch of the illustrious MacGregor
clan plays matchmaker again, this time to his three
gorgeous granddaughters in

THE MACGREGOR BRIDES

From Silhouette Books

Don't miss this brand-new continuation of Nora Roberts's
enormously popular *MacGregor* miniseries.

Available November 1997 at your favorite retail outlet.

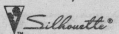

NRMB-S